Fright Camp

Look for more books in the Goosebumps Series 2000
by R.L. Stine:

#1 *Cry of the Cat*
#2 *Bride of the Living Dummy*
#3 *Creature Teacher*
#4 *Invasion of the Body Squeezers, Part I*
#5 *Invasion of the Body Squeezers, Part II*
#6 *I Am Your Evil Twin*
#7 *Revenge R Us*

Fright Camp

AN
APPLE
PAPERBACK

SCHOLASTIC INC.
New York Toronto London Auckland Sydney

A PARACHUTE PRESS BOOK

ISBN 0-590-39995-0

Copyright © 1998 by Parachute Press, Inc.
All rights reserved. Published by Scholastic Inc.
APPLE PAPERBACKS and logo are trademarks and/or registered trademarks of Scholastic Inc.
GOOSEBUMPS is a registered trademark of Parachute Press, Inc.

12 11 10 9 8 7 6 5 4 3 2 1   8 9/9 0 1 2 3/0

Printed in the U.S.A.   40

First Scholastic printing, August 1998

The Revenge of Dr. Cruel . . .
Carnival of Disgusting Horrors . . .
Crab Monsters versus the Leech People . . .
Do you love those movies too?

My brother, Tyler, and I bought the videos, and we watch them all the time. We love all scary movies. But those three movies were made by R.B. Farraday — and he is our favorite.

We watch his TV show — *Nightmare House* — every week. And we go to his movies and then buy them on video. I guess you figured it out — we are R.B. Farraday fans!

One day last winter, Dad came home with a big smile on his face. "I have something you might be interested in, Andrew," he said to me. He pulled a folded-up brochure from his overcoat pocket and handed it to me.

1

I unfolded it and read the big words on the front: R.B. FARRADAY'S FRIGHT CAMP.

I gazed at it in shock. "He — he's opening a summer camp?" I choked out.

Dad nodded.

I called Tyler in and held the brochure up in front of his face. "Huh? Can we go?" he cried. "Can we go this summer?"

Dad nodded again.

And then the whole Herman house went berserk. Tyler and I were leaping up and down, screaming at the top of our lungs. Mom and Dad were laughing.

What a happy moment.

"Let me see that!" Tyler cried. He tried to grab the camp brochure from my hand — and ripped it in two.

"Whoa! Easy, guys! Easy!" Dad warned.

"Just what a fright camp needs," Mom muttered. "Two more out-of-control monsters."

Mom always calls Tyler and me monsters when we get a little enthusiastic. I'm twelve and Tyler is ten. But she thinks we should act like adults at all times.

That would be kind of boring — wouldn't it?

After we stopped leaping around the house, screaming, and bouncing off the walls like pinballs, Dad helped us tape the brochure pages back together.

"I don't know, Andrew," he said, handing me the

brochure. "This camp looks pretty scary. You and Tyler might be too frightened."

I rolled my eyes. "For sure."

"Yeah. I'm shaking. I'm shaking!" Tyler exclaimed. He pretended to be scared, making his whole body quiver like Jell-O.

Tyler is good at that. He's skinny as a worm and very loose and acrobatic. We both have short, straight brown hair and round dark eyes. But I always look serious. And Tyler almost always looks goofy. He's always twisting himself up, making faces, making kids laugh.

But we were both serious as we studied the camp brochure. We were so excited, we couldn't speak.

The camp had *everything*! The Haunted Forest . . . the Lake of the Water Zombies . . .

Wow!

"How will we ever wait till July?" I cried.

"I wish I could close my eyes and it would be summer now!" Tyler declared.

Of course, we didn't have any way of knowing that the camp would be a little different from what we expected.

We had no way of knowing just how frightening Fright Camp would be.

And we had no way of knowing what was waiting for us there, deep, deep at the bottom of the Cavern of No Return.

2

"Whoa!"

Tyler and I cheered as the camp bus hit another bump and we all flew up out of our seats.

"Do you think R.B. Farraday designed this bus?" Meredith Friedman asked. She and her sister, Elizabeth, had the seat behind Tyler and me. We met them when we got on.

They seemed pretty nice. Except that Elizabeth kept popping blue bubblegum bubbles and spraying the back of my head with spit.

And Meredith kept calling me Andy. Nobody calls me Andy. Everyone calls me Andrew.

"The Camp Bus of No Return!" Tyler declared.

"No. *Revenge of the Speed Demon!"* Meredith suggested.

"*Camp Bus Monsters from Outer Space!*" Elizabeth cried.

We all stared at her. R.B. Farraday would never come up with a tacky title like that.

Elizabeth blushed.

The bus swerved around a curve. Nothing but flat farms out there. Mile after mile of green fields.

"Are we there yet?" a boy called from the back of the bus.

"Are we there yet? Are we there yet?"

We all began to chant it over and over.

Soon, tall trees replaced the flat fields. The highway curved into thick forest.

"They show a different R.B. Farraday movie every night," Meredith declared. "Isn't that cool?"

"Tyler and I have seen them all," I bragged. "At least six times."

"But I want to see them all again," Tyler chimed in.

Elizabeth suddenly looked worried. "It isn't *all* scary — is it?" she asked. "I mean, we get to do some normal camp things — right?"

Meredith snickered. "What do *you* want to do, Lizzy? Make beaded necklaces and origami animals in arts and crafts?"

Elizabeth blushed again. "Well . . ."

I opened my mouth to say something. But the bus jolted — and squealed — and slid hard.

I fell into the aisle.

I heard Tyler scream.

Other kids cried out.

I bounced on the floor as the bus skidded to a screeching stop.

Some kids were shouting in shock. Others were laughing.

I started to pull myself back up to my seat.

And I nearly fell again when I heard the driver utter an angry cry.

I heard gasps.

Turned to the front of the bus.

And saw someone force his way through the front bus door. A man in black — black from head to foot — a wide-brimmed black hat over a black mask, black sweatshirt over black pants.

"Hey — you're not supposed to be on here!" the driver screamed angrily.

The man in black growled something. I couldn't hear what he said.

"Get off — now!" the driver ordered.

The man reached out black-gloved hands. He grabbed the driver by the front of the shirt — and lifted him out of his seat.

"Hey!" the driver protested. He was a short, skinny guy and pretty old. He had white hair and wore thick glasses.

But he started wrestling with the man in black, grunting and groaning, trying to shove him back out the bus door.

Some kids were screaming. But Tyler and I watched in shocked silence.

My heart thudded in my chest. I could feel my throat tighten.

What was this about?

The two men banged against one side of the bus. Then wrestled up to the windshield. The driver's face was bright red. The man had him in a choke hold.

"Get away, kids!" the driver gasped. "Get away — fast!"

No one moved.

I stared in horror as the man in black lifted the scrawny bus driver off the floor — and heaved him out the bus door.

Through the window, I could see him roll off the pavement, onto the dirt at the side of the road. He landed facedown in the dirt — and didn't move.

I turned to the front. The man in black slid into the driver's seat. He slammed the bus door shut.

With a squeal of tires, the bus roared back onto the highway.

We hit a bump. I flew off the seat. My head crashed into the roof. I saw Tyler slam into the seat in front of us.

Kids were screaming. I heard a few kids crying.

"Stop it! Stop the bus!" a girl shrieked.

"Let us out!" the girl next to her demanded.

The bus swerved hard, sending several kids

tumbling into the aisle. Our new driver, hunched over the wheel, ignored all the screams and cries.

We picked up speed.

"Who is he?" Meredith cried, leaning over our seat-back. "Where is he taking us?"

3

A big truck roared past, honking its horn. We swerved again. Kids cried and screamed.

Suddenly, Tyler started to laugh.

"What's so f-funny?" Elizabeth stammered.

"Don't you get it?" Tyler cried. He had to shout over the screams of the kids. "It's all an act."

"Huh?" Gripping the seat-back, the two sisters gaped at him, openmouthed.

"Yes!" I cried happily. "Yes! I get it!" I grinned at my brother. "This is exactly what happened in *Vacation of Endless Doom*. A crazed zombie kidnaps a bus of campers and drives off with them forever. Drives and drives till the end of time — until the kids *actually* scream their heads off!"

"Right!" Tyler exclaimed. We slapped each other a high five.

"It's just an act," I told the two girls. "Part of the fun. We're probably getting close to camp."

The bus swerved hard again. Kids shrieked and begged the driver to stop.

"I really don't think it's fun," Meredith sniffed.

"It's a *fright* camp — remember?" Tyler said. "It's supposed to be frightening."

"But this is going too far," she insisted.

Her sister settled back in the seat, eyes shut, arms tightly crossed in front of her.

"It's all a joke," I told them again. "You watch. The guy in black is going to pull into the camp. Then he'll probably tear off his black mask and welcome us."

"Hey — check it out!" Tyler pointed out the window.

As we roared past the blur of trees, I saw a tall sign for the camp. It showed the Headless Ghoul. THIS WAY TO YOUR DOOM! it proclaimed in red letters. A green arrow, dripping like slime, pointed straight ahead.

"See?" I cried. "The driver is taking us right to Fright Camp. I *knew* it!"

"Are — are you sure?" Elizabeth stammered, still hugging herself.

"Of course," I replied. I pointed out the bouncing bus window. "Look — there's the entrance."

We all stared at the drippy green arrow, pointing to a wide driveway: ENTER HERE.

"Yessss!" Tyler and I slapped another high five.

10

A hush fell over the bus. Everyone stared out the window, watching for the driver to turn into the camp.

The huge green entrance arrow loomed up in front of us — and then it slid by our windows as we *sped past it*!

"Noooooo!" Loud groans rose over the roar of the bus.

"You missed the turn!" I shouted to the driver.

"Go back! Go back!" some kids shrieked.

I could see the entrance sign, shrinking smaller and smaller out the back window. We hit a hard bump and rumbled along the highway.

Hunched over the big wheel, the driver clicked on the loudspeaker. His voice boomed over the bus, low and evil:

"Sit back, kids. We're not going to camp. I have other plans for you!"

creams rang out. Cries of horror.

"Let us out!"

"Stop the bus!"

"Stop it! Stop! Where are we *going*?"

Tyler and I exchanged terrified glances. We were both so sure the whole thing was an act. But now the bus was carrying us farther and farther from the camp.

We both hunched down in the seat. My heart pounded so hard, I could barely breathe.

"Where is he taking us?" Tyler murmured.

Before I could answer, the bus swerved again. We were all thrown to the right as the bus turned sharply onto a gravel path.

The gravel crackled under the tires as we sped along the path. Tall, dark trees — a forest of trees — bounced past on both sides.

"He — he's taking us deep into the forest," I heard Elizabeth stammer in a tiny voice.

But suddenly, the trees ended. The bus bounced into a flat green field.

A long, wood rail fence stretched across the field. I could see low cabins and other buildings on a sloping hill beyond the fence.

And then a wide gate. And a painted sign above the gate: WELCOME TO FRIGHT CAMP.

"Huh?" I cried. "Are we really at camp?"

The bus finally slowed. It pulled to a stop in front of a long wooden building that looked like a big log cabin.

The driver sat up straight and clicked on the loudspeaker again. "Welcome to Fright Camp, everyone. Did I give you a scare?"

"Yes!" everyone cried. I heard loud sighs of relief. I started to laugh. I couldn't keep it in. A lot of kids were laughing now.

I glanced around the bus. Some kids had grown very pale. Some had tear stains on their cheeks. Two girls were *still* crying.

"This is the *real* entrance to the camp," the driver announced. "That other entrance sign back on the highway is a phony."

He pulled off his black mask. He was a young guy with short blond hair and two teeth that stuck out of his mouth. He looked like a rabbit.

"Hope I gave you a good scare." He grinned. "Of

13

course, this was just the first." His grin grew wider. "It gets a lot scarier than this."

Several counselors were waiting to welcome us. They all wore green shorts and T-shirts, the color of green slime.

I jumped off the bus and stretched my arms and legs. It felt so good to breathe fresh air. And to be off that bus!

As I followed the others to the big log cabin — the main lodge — I gazed around.

Wow!

Down the hill, I could see a Spin-and-Scream ride. "That must be the ride from *Carnival of Disgusting Horrors*," I told Tyler.

He didn't hear me. He was talking to two other kids from the bus. They were pointing excitedly at the go-cart track back near the trees.

That's the track from *Go-carts from the Evil Kingdom*, I told myself.

I was so excited I could barely walk! Being here at Fright Camp was like living in one of R.B. Farraday's movies!

Squinting in the bright sunlight, I saw rows of small cabins and buildings. They led down to a sandy beach and a sparkling blue lake.

Is that the Lake of the Water Zombies? I wondered.

"What movie do you think they'll show tonight?" a kid behind me asked.

14

"Do we get to go swimming? I'm hot."

"Do you think R.B. Farraday is here?"

"He's supposed to be. It said so in the brochure."

"Will we get to meet him?"

"Are those real caves in those rocks?"

Excited voices all around me. I wanted to run around and see and do everything. But the counselors herded us into the lodge.

We had to register and sign up for activities. I chose movie appreciation, swimming, and horror poster art.

I searched for Tyler and saw him way behind me in line. He was still talking to the two guys from the bus. Meredith and Elizabeth were behind him. I could see them arguing about what activities to choose.

We had to sign a bunch of papers. Then we had to check off the foods we liked on a long list and fill out a form for the camp nurse.

Finally, we were assigned cabins. Tyler and I were assigned to Cabin Three. I found it, about halfway down the hill toward the lake. The cabin was small — two bunk beds and two dressers.

Kids had already claimed the bunk by the window. They had stuff piled on the bed and on the dresser beside it. I wondered who our roommates were.

"Hey, Andrew, when do we get to explore?"

Tyler asked. "Do you think we can ride the go-carts whenever we want?"

I finished stuffing my clothes into a drawer. Then I shoved my camp trunk under our bunk. "Let's go find out," I replied, wiping sweat off my forehead.

We stepped out of the cabin and bumped into a counselor. He was tall — very tall — and very skinny. He looked like a broom handle with blond hair on top.

"Hey, guys," he greeted us. "I'm Gus. I'm the counselor for Cabin Three." He had a nice smile.

Tyler and I introduced ourselves.

"Cabin Three rocks!" Gus exclaimed enthusiastically. "Cabin Three *rules*! Did you meet Jack and Chris? They're your bunk mates. Why don't you do some exploring? Have a look around."

"Okay!" Tyler and I cried out happily. We started down the hill.

"Just one thing!" Gus called after us.

We turned back to him.

"Don't go into the Cavern of No Return," he warned. His blue eyes flashed. "Know why?"

I took a guess. "Because we won't return?"

Gus laughed. "You got it."

Then his smile faded. "Be careful, guys. Really," he said, lowering his voice. "This camp . . . well . . . it isn't what it seems."

"Huh? What do you mean?" Tyler demanded.

16

But Gus didn't reply. He turned and trotted up the path toward the lodge.

Tyler and I spun around, trying to decide which direction to go first. Down the row of cabins, kids were still dragging their suitcases and trunks. Excited voices floated over the warm summer air.

A few guys had started a tetherball game around a pole near the top of the hill. I saw a group of girls talking and laughing outside their cabin door.

Tyler and I followed a path toward the trees. I bent to swat a bug on my leg.

When I stood up, I saw that we were in front of a sign — arrows pointing in all directions to different areas of the camp.

THE HAUNTED FOREST —
STRAIGHT AHEAD.
LAKE OF THE WATER ZOMBIES —
TO THE RIGHT.
BOTTOMLESS QUICKSAND PIT OF
SCREAMS —
TO THE LEFT.
THE MINE OF LOST SOULS . . . THE CAVERN
OF NO RETURN . . . GHOST CABIN . . .

Arrows pointed left and right.

"Wow! Everything from R.B. Farraday's

movies!" Tyler exclaimed. "It's all here! And we're *in* it!"

I opened my mouth to reply — but a shrill cry made me stop.

I spun around. Tyler heard it too.

A scream.

"Help me — somebody!" A boy's terrified voice. "Please — help me!"

5

e both turned toward the trees.

I saw a red-haired boy. His hand — it was stuck in something. Something round and white.

"Help me!"

Tyler and I raced toward him.

The boy squirmed and struggled.

His hand — it was caught in a wasps' nest!

I could hear the angry buzz of the wasps.

The boy twisted and pulled. But he couldn't free his hand.

"Ohhhh, help! Help!" he moaned. "They're stinging me! They're stinging me!"

Tyler and I ran across the grass. I turned and saw two others running after us. Meredith and Elizabeth.

Gasping for breath, we all reached the boy at the same time.

"What's happening?" Elizabeth cried. "How did he *do* that?"

"Just *help!*" the boy groaned.

He struggled and squirmed. Sweat poured down his face. His red hair was matted wetly to his forehead.

He gave a hard tug, but the hand wouldn't come free.

"It — it's swollen from all the stings," he moaned.

"Let me try," I said. I took a deep breath. Then I raised both hands — and grabbed the sides of the wasps' nest.

"Go ahead — pull out your hand," I instructed him.

The wasps buzzed angrily inside the white nest.

Please don't sting me, I thought. Please!

The buzzing rose to a roar. My hands trembled. I gripped the wasps' nest tightly, my eyes shut, every muscle tensed.

"Hurry! Pull!" I pleaded. "I'm holding it."

A smile crossed the boy's face. He slid his hand out easily.

He held it up.

Not red or swollen. No stings.

He tossed back his head and laughed.

We all uttered startled cries. I pulled the wasps' nest closer to examine it.

Plastic.

I peered inside. The angry buzzing sound came from a tiny speaker.

"It's a joke," the boy said. "My friend and I discovered it this morning."

"Aaaaggh!" I uttered an angry cry — and swung the wasps' nest as hard as I could. The tree branch swung with it. The plastic nest was wired to the tree.

The boy introduced himself. His name was Jack Harding. He wore black shorts and a gray T-shirt with FRIGHT CAMP in dripping bloodred letters.

"My friend Chris and I got here this morning," he told us, smoothing back his red hair.

"Are you in Cabin Three?" I asked.

He nodded.

"We're in the same cabin!" I declared. "So is Tyler."

"Cool," Jack replied. "I've been exploring all day. This camp is awesome — especially if you like scary stuff."

"Of *course* we like scary stuff," Meredith replied. "Why else would we come to a fright camp?"

"But is *everything* fake?" Elizabeth demanded.

Before Jack could answer, another boy stepped out of the woods. He had long black hair pulled back into a ponytail. He was big and athletic-looking and also wore a Fright Camp T-shirt over baggy shorts.

"Hey," Jack greeted him. "This is my friend Christian Kretschmer."

"You can call me Chris," he said, pulling a bug out of his black hair and flicking it at Jack. A *real* bug.

"I pulled the wasp joke," Jack told him. "They fell for it."

Chris snickered. "Cool."

"Chris and I have been all over this place," Jack said. He pulled up a long blade of grass from the ground and began sucking on it.

"So — is everything a fake?" Elizabeth repeated. "Is it all just a joke?"

Jack's smile faded. "Not everything," he replied, moving the grass blade around in his mouth.

"That's what's so scary about this camp," Chris added. "Some of it is real."

"Like what?" Tyler asked.

The two boys hesitated. They glanced at each other.

"Maybe you should find out for yourselves," Chris said quietly.

"No — tell us," I insisted. "What's real?"

"Well . . ." Jack pulled the blade of grass from his mouth and tossed it to the ground. "Over there," he said. "That's real." He pointed.

I saw a wide circle of yellow sand cut into the grass. A wooden sign stood beside it, but I couldn't read the words.

"It's the quicksand pit," Chris said.

"Huh? It's real?" I cried.

Jack and Chris both nodded.

"We heard that a counselor got caught in it last week, before camp opened," Chris said in a whisper. His eyes darted tensely back and forth. "The poor guy. He got sucked right down."

"You're kidding," I said.

I studied their solemn faces.

"You're kidding — right?" I demanded. "That's another joke — right?"

Jack glanced nervously at the quicksand pit. "We'll see. . . ."

Tyler and I explored a little while longer. We checked out the beach and the lake. But I kept glancing back at the quicksand pit.

Was Jack pulling another joke on us?

Tyler ran to join the kids he'd met on the bus. As I started back to the cabin, I heard whistles blowing.

"Camp meeting in the lodge!" a green-uniformed counselor called out. "All campers to the lodge!"

Kids came jogging in from all directions. I waved to Jack and Chris as I made my way through the open doorway.

The front of the lodge was built to look like a log cabin. But the building was actually two stories tall and as big as a barn.

To the left, I could see a row of small rooms

down a long hallway. We were herded into an enormous room with wooden rafters along the ceiling and tall stone fireplaces on both ends. Long wooden tables filled the center of the room. A sign proclaimed: MESS HALL & MEETING ROOM.

Movie posters of R.B. Farraday films were hung along one wall. I recognized *The Beast with Three Brains* and *Kunga, the Animal Vampire.*

The counselors motioned for us to sit at the long tables. I found a seat in the second row of tables next to some older-looking guys.

I started to say something to them. But a tall, athletic-looking counselor stepped in front of us. "Both hands on the tables, guys," he instructed. "Fast. Hands on the tables."

"Whoa!" I uttered a startled cry as he pulled up heavy black cords from under the table — and strapped them around our wrists.

"Handcuffs?" one of the other kids cried.

"Are we under arrest?" someone called.

We all laughed at that.

But I felt a little strange as counselors moved quickly along the tables, strapping down everyone's hands.

And a chill tingled the back of my neck as I felt a hum of electricity run through the black cords.

"What is *this* about?" I asked the guy next to me.

He shrugged. "It's pretty weird," he muttered.

I tugged at the cords. They were fastened tight. I couldn't slip free.

Again, I felt a hum of electricity around my wrists.

I turned and glanced behind me. I saw Meredith and Elizabeth at the next table. Their wrists were strapped down. They were chatting excitedly, both talking at once.

In the row behind them, I saw Chris struggling with the counselors. "No way!" he shouted. "No way!"

He wrapped his hands behind his back and jumped to his feet. "You can't do this!" he cried angrily.

But three counselors held Chris down. They pulled his hands apart and strapped his wrists. "A troublemaker," one of the counselors said. "What's your name? We're going to remember you."

"I don't believe this," I muttered to the boy next to me. "Why is Chris so frightened?"

The boy shrugged. "Beats me."

I didn't have long to think about it. A big, tough-looking man in a white lab coat stepped to the front of the room. He raised two enormous hands to silence us.

"Welcome — prisoners!" he bellowed.

We all laughed. Uncomfortable laughter.

Two counselors rushed up to him. They both pointed to Chris. The man in the lab coat stared long and hard at Chris.

The man had cold gray eyes and a broad, bulby nose that looked as if it had been broken several times. He was nearly bald. A dark scar started at one eyebrow and trailed up along his forehead.

He raised his hands until the room grew silent. "My name is Alonso," he announced. "I am the assistant warden."

Warden? Prisoners?

What's going on here? I wondered.

But then I saw a smile spread over Alonso's face. His gray eyes twinkled. "Welcome to Fright Camp, everyone!" he declared. He rubbed his hands together. "We are going to do our best to give you some good scares this summer."

"Why are our hands strapped down?" a boy demanded in an angry, trembling voice. I turned and saw that it was Jack.

"Yeah! Let us go!" Chris cried angrily. "You can't do this! Let us go!"

I felt a tingle of electricity against my wrists.

Alonso glared at my two bunk mates. "What are your names?" he demanded.

Jack and Chris didn't reply.

"Your names?" Alonso repeated, lumbering toward them menacingly.

The two boys called out their names.

"And what cabin are you in?" Alonso asked.

They both hesitated. "Cabin Three," Chris told him finally.

A strange, unpleasant grin spread over Alonso's face. The scar on his forehead throbbed. "That will be our *lucky* cabin," he declared coldly.

27

lonso turned and strode back to the front of the room. "I have a wonderful treat for you now," he announced in his deep, booming voice. "I have the pleasure of introducing the owner of Fright Camp. His thirty-five movies have won him the title of Scariest Man on Earth! Let's give a big Fright Camp welcome to R.B. Farraday!"

I tried to clap, but the tight cords around my wrists made it hard. So I cheered instead.

We all cheered and screamed as R.B. Farraday shuffled into the room. I heard a few kids gasp in surprise. He wasn't the way we pictured him.

For one thing, he was very short. He only came up to Alonso's shoulders. He wasn't just short. He was tiny. A small, slender head topped with slicked-down black hair. A closely trimmed black beard with a streak of gray down the center.

He wore a black T-shirt, black shorts, and sandals. His legs were skinny as toothpicks. So were his arms.

I saw something sparkle against the front of his shirt. Squinting, I saw that it was a silvery skull on a chain, with glittering red eyes.

I leaned over the table, staring at him. My hero! The most famous horror director on Earth. I couldn't believe I was in the same room as he was!

Mr. Farraday pulled himself onto a tall wooden stool. He had a clipboard in one hand. He scratched his beard with the other hand, waiting for our cheers to stop.

"Thank you for the warm welcome," he said finally. I leaned forward, straining to listen. He had a soft, almost whispery voice.

"This is an exciting summer for me," he continued. He spread the clipboard across his bony knees. "As Alonso told you, I've made thirty-five movies. But that's only film. Color images on celluloid. This camp gives me a chance to bring my movies to life. And now, you will all be actors!"

We cheered again.

The cords tugged at my wrist. "Why are we wearing these?" I called out.

Several other kids chimed in. The big room echoed with our questions.

Alonso signaled sternly for us to be quiet.

But Mr. Farraday rubbed his beard and smiled. "Have any of you seen my film *The Revenge of Dr. Cruel?*" he asked.

Several kids cried out yes.

"Then you will recognize the Fear Meter," Mr. Farraday said. "These wires connect all of you to the actual Fear Meter that was used in the movie."

"But — what does it do?" a girl called from the front row.

"I will show you," Mr. Farraday replied. He slid down from the stool and turned to Alonso. "Why don't you pick a volunteer?"

Alonso rumbled up to the tables. He fiddled with the cuffs of his white lab coat. His gray eyes swept back and forth over the room.

He really looks like an evil doctor in one of R.B. Farraday's movies, I thought.

I hadn't seen *The Revenge of Dr. Cruel* in a long time. I struggled to remember exactly what the Fear Meter did.

Alonso raised a big hand and pointed. "Let's demonstrate on that one," Alonso said. "One of the troublemakers."

"No!" I heard Chris scream. "No — not me!" He struggled to free his hands from the cords. "Please! Not me!"

Why is he so afraid? I wondered.

Kids shifted and squirmed. All eyes were on Chris now.

I caught the frightened expressions on Elizabeth's and Meredith's faces. Behind them, Jack had his eyes shut tight.

I turned back to the front and saw Mr. Farraday push some buttons on a control panel. Then he threw a big switch on the wall.

"Nooooo!" Chris gasped.

I heard a sharp crackle of electricity.

Chris jerked hard in his seat.

His head snapped back.

He jumped up. His whole body twisted and danced.

Another hard jolt of electricity.

Kids screamed. Horrified cries shook the room.

I let out a laugh. "It's a joke," I told the boy next to me. "It's got to be a joke."

But Chris's head snapped to one side. And then his whole body collapsed.

He crumpled onto the table and didn't move.

"Shut it down! Shut it down!" Mr. Farraday screamed. He fiddled frantically with the control buttons.

Alonso leaned over Chris and shook him by the shoulders.

Some kids screamed. Others stared in silence. I gasped for breath, my heart pounding, watching Alonso try to revive Chris.

"Is he okay?" Mr. Farraday demanded. "Is he alive?"

"He'll survive," Alonso replied coldly. He motioned to two counselors. "Take him out of here."

Alonso loosened the straps. The two counselors lifted Chris's limp body from the seat. They had a lot of trouble pulling him up and almost dropped him.

No one uttered a sound as the counselors carried Chris from the room. The door closed hard behind them.

Mr. Farraday rubbed his beard and paced back and forth in front of the fireplace. He motioned for Alonso to join him.

"We'd better turn down the voltage for the next group," Mr. Farraday told his assistant, shaking his head.

Alonso rubbed his hands together. An evil smile crossed his face. "It's more fun this way!" he declared.

Mr. Farraday stopped pacing and stared at him. "You're too evil, Alonso. Don't make me sorry I hired you for this job."

Alonso's grin grew wider. "Don't make me sorry I *took* the job," he shot back.

Mr. Farraday shook his head again. "Maybe I should have left you rotting in that prison cell. Maybe you *haven't* changed after all."

Huh? Prison cell? I thought. I swallowed hard. Why is Mr. Farraday saying all this? Has he forgotten we can all hear him?

"Is Chris okay?" Jack called from the back of the room. "Is he going to be okay?"

Mr. Farraday and Alonso glared angrily at each other and didn't reply.

"Will you take these cords off our wrists now?" a girl down the table from me asked.

Her question appeared to snap Mr. Farraday from his thoughts. He suddenly remembered we were all sitting there. But he didn't answer her.

"Sorry, boys and girls," he said instead. "My fright camp is brand-new. So we're still working out a few problems." He narrowed his eyes again at Alonso. "Problems like you," he added coldly.

Alonso's face turned bright red. He uttered an angry growl. The deep scar on his forehead darkened to purple.

"Go wheel in our special guest," Mr. Farraday ordered him.

He turned back to us. "Isn't it strange?" he said softly. "What happened to that boy Chris is exactly what happened in *The Revenge of Dr. Cruel.* So strange . . ."

He drifted off into his own thoughts again, shaking his head.

He reminded me of a grasshopper as he climbed back onto the high stool. He was so wiry and thin.

"Lots of kids think my camp is a fake," he told us, tapping one hand against the clipboard. He leaned toward us. "But I think horror has to be *real.*"

He seemed to stare right at me. His dark eyes burned into mine.

"I think horror has to be real — or else it isn't scary," he said in a low whisper.

I felt a shudder of fear.

Is he just saying that to put us in the mood? I wondered.

Or is he *crazy*?

stared back at Mr. Farraday, waiting for him to crack a smile. Waiting for him to admit that Chris was only acting, that the jolt of electricity wasn't real, that it was all a joke.

But his expression remained solemn.

A low, rumbling sound made me turn to the doors at the back of the room. The cords strained at my wrists.

The doors swung open.

First I saw metal bars. A cage. And then I saw a big, dark figure huddled inside the cage.

Alonso and another counselor pushed the cage up to the front of the room.

A gorilla!

Big black eyes poked out from chocolate-brown fur. The gorilla gripped the bars of the cage with both hands. And bounced up and down, making grunting sounds.

Is it real?

That was my first question.

It looked so human, gripping the bars with its furry fingers. Staring out at us as the cage rolled to the front of the room.

The creature's mouth dropped open, and a purple tongue flopped out. It uttered a loud grunt, as if it recognized Mr. Farraday.

It's a real gorilla, I realized. It's not a man in a costume.

The animal pulled itself up straight as Alonso spun the cage around to face us. It snarled loudly and pounded the bars with two fists.

Some little kids at the front table screamed.

Mr. Farraday remained on the tall stool. He watched the snarling animal warily. Then he turned to us.

"This is our special guest at Fright Camp," he announced. "You're probably surprised to see a gorilla at a summer camp. Well, I've planned a lot of surprises for you."

"Is that Rocko?" Tyler called out.

Mr. Farraday smiled. "You recognize him! Very good! How many of you have seen my movie *Conquerors of the Gorilla Planet*?"

I tried to raise my hand, but the cord tugged it back down. Excited murmurs rose up around the room. That was one of R.B. Farraday's most popular movies.

The gorilla's fur bristled. It didn't seem to like the noise. It opened its mouth in another angry snarl and pounded both fists against the bars.

"Rocko was the leading man in that movie," Mr. Farraday continued. "He was our best actor too. We never had to tell him to get scarier. And he worked for peanuts!"

The gorilla jumped up and down and then tilted its big head back in a roar.

Mr. Farraday turned to Alonso. "Be careful with him," he ordered. "Rocko is pretty vicious. He mangled his handler last week. He put the poor guy in the hospital."

The gorilla roared again.

"Rocko hasn't adapted well to captivity," Mr. Farraday told us. "Gorillas have been known to —"

The movie director stopped in midsentence. His mouth dropped open. The clipboard fell from his hand. "Hey!"

With another roar, the gorilla shot both arms forward — and swung open the cage door.

"Alonso — you idiot!" Mr. Farraday shrieked. "You left the cage door open! Close it! *Close it!*"

Alonso dove to the cage door.

Too late.

Roaring furiously, the gorilla burst out of the cage. Its feet slapped the floor hard. It swung its arms wildly in front of it, as if clearing a path for itself.

"Stop it! Stop it!" Mr. Farraday's cries rose up over the shrill screams of the campers.

Snarling, the gorilla turned its head quickly from side to side, peering down the long table.

Alonso leaped onto the animal's back. But it shrugged him off easily, like shaking off a fly. Alonso toppled heavily to the floor.

Mr. Farraday slid off the stool and backed away, backed up till he hit the fireplace. "Stop it! Somebody!" he cried. "It's a killer! The gorilla — it's a killer!"

A scream escaped my throat. The room rang out with shrieks and cries.

I tried to jump up. I saw several kids struggling to get away.

But we were all strapped down to the tables.

We couldn't move.

The gorilla stepped over Alonso. Lumbered up to my table. Spread out its massive arms.

"Nooooo!"

I let out a shrill, terrified scream as its heavy hands closed around me.

10

I ducked low as the gorilla swung its arms together.

I felt a whoosh of air above my head. The fur on one gorilla arm brushed the top of my head.

"Ohhhhhhhh." A low moan escaped my throat.

I glanced up and saw the big creature lumbering away down the table. It swiped at another boy. And then it tossed back its head and let out another roar that shook the rafters.

I heard a cry — and spun my head in time to see a tall, lanky, green-uniformed counselor burst through the door.

"Duck down, everybody!" he called frantically. He raised a rifle to his shoulder.

Screams. Cries of horror.

Chairs scraped against the concrete floor as we all ducked.

"No!" I heard Mr. Farraday protest shrilly. "Carl — don't shoot him! It's a valuable gorilla! Don't!"

The counselor took aim.

An explosion ripped through the screams and terrified cries.

The gorilla uttered a startled groan. Its big arms shot out at its sides. Its mouth dropped open. Its dark eyes bulged.

The animal uttered a high, whining cry. It grabbed at its chest.

And then it fell forward. Fell with a heavy *THUD*.

Dropped to the floor — and didn't move.

The room grew silent. A few kids were still screaming. I heard some kids crying.

I pulled myself back into my seat. The cords strained at my wrists. I could still feel the brush of the gorilla's arm on the top of my head.

Chill after chill swept down my spine. I couldn't stop shaking. I gasped for breath.

Alonso and two counselors huddled over the gorilla. Alonso tugged something off the gorilla's chest and handed it to the movie director.

A dart.

"A tranquilizer dart," Mr. Farraday announced, holding it high so everyone could see it. "We would never harm the best actor in our studio!"

He laughed.

Kids groaned and sighed in relief.

"Good job, everyone," Mr. Farraday declared.

Alonso and the counselors got the gorilla up on its feet. Its big head rolled around groggily on its shoulders. They pushed the dazed creature back into its cage.

"Did we give you a good scare?" Mr. Farraday grinned. "Did we make you *believe*?"

Counselors moved up and down the tables, freeing our wrists from the cords.

My heart was still pounding. Sweat poured down my forehead. My T-shirt stuck wetly to my back.

"Believe!" Mr. Farraday cried, his eyes wild, gesturing with both hands. "Believe in *terror*!"

I stared at him, studying him. How far will he go to scare us? I wondered.

How *real* will the terror be?

I didn't have to wait long to find out.

Tyler and I went back to our cabin and finished unpacking. I taped up a few posters on the wall beside my bed. But they didn't help cheer me up.

I still felt frightened and tense.

Tyler hunched on the edge of his bed, his arms crossed tightly in front of his chest. He hadn't said a word. He had chewed his bottom lip, and now it was bleeding. He does that a lot when he's scared.

"Maybe we should go home," he said finally. "Maybe this place is too scary. Farraday seems kind of crazy — doesn't he?"

I shrugged. "You know we can't go home. You

know Mom and Dad are away until August. Besides, it's all supposed to be fun," I said. "I think Farraday was acting."

"But that gorilla was *real*," Tyler insisted. "And so was the electric current in the cords. I felt it humming. And then it really jolted Chris."

"Maybe that was an accident," I suggested.

"That Alonso guy is so scary," my brother muttered.

I glanced down at him. Tyler looked so small and pitiful hugging himself like that, it made me laugh. "Hey, lighten up!" I cried. "This is Fright Camp — right? It's just what you'd expect from R.B. Farraday, the Scariest Man on Earth!"

"I — I guess," Tyler stammered in a tiny voice.

"We didn't want to go to an ordinary summer camp — remember? This is going to be exciting," I insisted.

Tyler sighed. He rested his head on his fists.

The cabin door swung open. Jack burst in, breathing hard. He wiped sweat off his forehead with the back of his hand.

Tyler jumped up from his lower bunk. "Is Chris okay?" he asked.

"I — I don't think so," Jack stammered. He swallowed hard and struggled to catch his breath. "I went to the infirmary to see him. He's messed up. He isn't right."

"Huh?" I gasped. "What do you mean?"

"He's talking crazy!" Jack cried. "He doesn't

43

make any sense. I think . . . I think the electric shock messed up his brain."

"It was *real*?" I cried. "It wasn't a fake?"

Jack shook his head. "I warned you. Chris and I heard things when we arrived this morning. Frightening things."

He lowered his voice. Tyler and I moved closer to hear him.

"I think it's really dangerous here," Jack continued. "We have to stick together. The four of us. They've got their eyes on us. They're watching Cabin Three. You see, Chris and I —"

He stopped with a gasp.

He stared over my shoulder to the window.

I turned — and saw a face in the window. Alonso.

Alonso, staring coldly in at us. Listening. Spying on us.

I turned back to Jack. His whole body shook. His face had lost all its color.

"I didn't say anything," Jack whispered. "If anyone asks, I didn't say a word."

And then he pushed past me and bolted out of the cabin.

I glanced back at the window. Alonso had vanished.

Tyler and I stared at each other. "Weird," Tyler murmured softly.

"Yeah. Weird," I replied.

44

What did Jack start to tell us? I wondered. And why was he so afraid of Alonso?

Jack shook all over. He was totally terrified.

"Weird," I repeated to Tyler.

And then I heard a shout. "Let me go!" a boy cried. "Please — please — let me go!"

12

We both dove for the cabin door. I got there first and leaped outside.

I ran out onto the path. Tyler came hurrying up behind me.

We both stared up the hill at Chris.

He was sprinting wildly across the grass. Running in crazy zigzags. Waving his arms. Whinnying. His head tossed back. Whinnying like a horse.

As I gaped in shock, I saw people chasing after him. Two counselors. And the camp nurse.

One of the counselors leaped into the air and tried to tackle Chris from behind.

But Chris made a sharp cut. Whinnying, he spun around and ran back up the hill.

"Let me go!" he shrieked again. "I won't tell anyone what I saw! I promise!"

Two counselors tackled him. They pulled him to his feet — and dragged him away.

Chris returned to our cabin after dinner. He seemed okay. Tyler and I asked him what had happened.

He turned away from us. "I don't want to talk about it," he murmured. I saw his whole body tremble. "Please, guys. Don't mention it again — okay?"

We didn't say another word. But I kept glancing at Chris all night, wondering why they were chasing him. And what they did to him after they caught him.

After lights out, I watched him sitting up in his top bunk, staring out the window for hours. Staring up at the moon, his expression grim, his body still as a statue.

It rained early the next morning. We all watched an R.B. Farraday movie. It was pretty good — and it took my mind off Chris.

When the sun came out just before lunch, the grass sparkled like diamonds. The camp appeared fresh and new, as if the rain had cleaned everything in sight.

Tyler and I had Free Time in the afternoon. Gus, our cabin counselor, called us aside. "The Spin-and-Scream ride is ready, if you want to try it out," he told us.

He didn't have to ask me twice.

I love rides — the faster the better. I love the feeling of zooming or spinning out of control.

I think roller coasters and other thrill rides are like scary movies. You feel as if you're really facing danger. But you know you'll be perfectly okay when the thrills are over.

Tyler doesn't like rides as much as I do. He followed me down the hill to the Spin-and-Scream ride. But I could tell by the way he kept close to me that he was a little afraid.

"Hurry!" I cried. I could see other kids running down to the ride. The little red-and-blue cars were filling up. I waved to Meredith and Elizabeth, but they didn't see me.

Tyler and I climbed into the last empty car. I pulled the safety bar down over our laps.

"Do you think it spins real fast?" Tyler asked in a tiny voice. He gripped the safety bar tightly with both hands.

"Probably not too fast," I replied. "But I'll bet it spins a lot." I grabbed a wheel on the side. "See? You turn this to make the car spin."

He pushed my hands from the wheel. "Don't make it spin too hard — okay?"

A big red-haired guy named Duffy was running the ride. I'd seen him early in the morning working out with weights in the exercise cabin. He had huge biceps that bulged out from under a red muscle shirt. He wore tight black spandex bike shorts that showed off his powerful legs.

48

I guessed he wasn't a counselor since he didn't wear the green T-shirt-and-shorts uniform. His whole job is running the ride, I figured.

Duffy came up to Tyler and me to check the safety bar. I saw a big blue-and-red tattoo of a grinning skull on his arm.

"Remember this ride in the movie?" he growled.

"You mean *Carnival of Disgusting Horrors*?" I replied. "Yeah. I remember it."

"Know why it's called the Spin-and-Scream?" Duffy asked, flashing a toothy smile. He laughed. "You'll find out."

We watched him walk over to the controls. He grabbed a long wooden lever and pushed it forward.

The cars squeaked and groaned and then started to move. I counted twelve cars, all filled with campers. We began to spin in a wide circle.

"This is cool!" Tyler declared. "What's so scary about this ride?"

"Nothing. It's just fun!" I declared.

We began to move faster. I spun the wheel and made our car twirl. Then I threw my hands up above my head and let out a happy cry.

The wind blew my hair into my face. The car began to whirl faster.

"Whoooooa! I'm dizzy!" I exclaimed.

Tyler gripped the safety bar with both hands. He had a tight grin stuck on his face. I could see he was trying to enjoy the ride. But his eyes were shut, and his face was starting to get pale.

Faster. Faster.

The cars whirled faster, creaking and groaning. The cabins, the trees, the lake — all became a bright, sparkling blur.

We whipped around hard, spinning, twirling.

I flew into Tyler. He gripped the bar, gritting his teeth.

Faster. Faster.

I saw Duffy push the long lever down all the way.

"Whoooooa!" I screamed. "We're flying now! We're *flying*!"

Kids screamed and laughed.

"Whooooa!" As we whipped around, I saw Duffy turn away from the controls. I spun my head — and saw him lumbering away, heading up the hill toward the lodge.

I felt so dizzy. Everything swirled past in a bright, fuzzy blur.

I blinked. Blinked again.

"Hey!" I called out to him.

But my voice came out weak. No way it could be heard over the shouts and squeals of the kids on the ride.

"Hey — where's he going?" Tyler demanded, squeezing my arm. I saw my brother's face twist in panic. "Where's he going, Andrew? Isn't he going to stop this thing?"

50

The air whipped my face. My hair blew wildly. I lowered my hands to the safety bar and held on.

We whipped around, faster . . . faster.

I fell against Tyler again. Then the car rocked me hard into the other side.

"Oww!" I cried out as I hit my arm. Then I bounced up out of the seat. The safety bar caught me. I fell back down.

I searched for Duffy. But he had vanished into the spinning green-and-blue blur.

No one there. No one at the controls.

Kids squealed and screamed.

"Stop this thing! Somebody — stop it!"

"It's too fast!"

"I feel sick!"

I started to feel sick too. My stomach lurched.

My mouth tasted sour. I could feel my lunch rising up to my throat.

Dizzy . . . so dizzy . . .

"Where is that guy?"

"He can't just leave us here — *can* he?"

Tyler was squeezing my leg. His eyes were shut. His mouth hung open in fear.

We seemed to spin even faster. My head jerked back on my neck. My shoulder slammed into the side of the car.

Over the screams, I could hear a few kids crying now. I heard a loud groan and saw a splash of yellow. One kid *did* lose his lunch.

I swallowed hard. I really felt sick now.

I shut my eyes to make the dizziness fade, but it didn't help.

"Ohhhhhh." I opened my mouth in a weak moan of horror.

How long would we spin? How long?

We whipped around again. Again.

Another kid sent a balloon of yellow vomit into the air.

Faster . . .

And then I saw a blurred figure in red and blue. Duffy.

As our car flew around again, I saw him coming back down the hill. Walking slowly . . . so slowly.

Kids groaned and cried. "Hurry!" someone screamed. "Please — hurry!"

We whipped around again.

Duffy had a red soda can in his hand. He tilted his head back and took a long drink. Then he began slowly making his way toward us again.

We spun around. Again. Again.

I held my breath.

Finally! Duffy stepped up to the controls.

We spun around again. Tyler's head bounced on his shoulders. His eyes were shut tight.

"Tyler — are you okay?" I gasped. "Tyler?"

He didn't answer.

We whirled around again.

I saw Duffy grab the lever.

Finally. Finally . . .

I watched him tug the lever.

"No!" I heard Duffy cry out.

And I saw the lever break off in his hands.

"**N**ooooo!" Horrified groans and cries of terror rose up from the whirling, spinning cars.

We roared around again.

I saw Duffy holding the broken lever in one hand. Scratching his head. Staring at it.

"Turn it off! Turn it off!"

"Help us!"

"Do something!"

Angry, terrified voices rang out over the roar of the spinning cars.

"Tyler? Are you okay?" I shook my brother. Shook him hard by the shoulder.

He opened his eyes, then closed them again. Bouncing hard on the metal seat, hunched over the safety bar.

The ground tilted up. I saw the sky crash into

the grass. The green grass and the blue sky appeared to trade places.

I'm going to faint, I realized.

My head fell back.

I shut my eyes.

And felt the car slowing down.

The roar of the motor cut off. We were spinning silently now, the air whooshing past, the metal cars creaking.

Slower . . . Slower . . .

I opened my eyes. I saw Duffy holding a heavy cord. Holding a plug. He had unplugged the ride.

We slowed to a stop.

No one moved. No one moved for the longest time.

And then kids began to climb out.

Some dropped to their hands and knees on the grass. Others staggered weakly, holding their heads, groaning and muttering angrily.

I helped pull Tyler from the car. His knees started to buckle. I held him up till he caught his balance.

Then we tried to walk. The ground tilted. Trees swayed in front of me as if they were rubber.

I bumped right into Meredith and Elizabeth.

"That was *horrible!*" Elizabeth cried.

Duffy loomed over us, a big grin on his face. "Enjoy the ride?" he asked, his pale blue eyes flashing merrily.

"I'm going to complain!" Meredith snapped. "I'm going to complain to Mr. Farraday!"

"Me too!" her sister agreed.

Duffy shook his head. "Didn't you see the movie?" he asked.

"I don't *care* about the movie!" Elizabeth snarled. "That was horrible! You made us all sick!"

"But that's exactly what happened in the movie!" Duffy declared. "This is Fright Camp — remember? The movies come to life!"

I remembered the scene in the movie now. The Spin-and-Scream kept whirling faster and faster — until all of the riders lost their skin! When the ride finally stopped, the cars were filled with skeletons.

"At least we didn't lose our skin," I muttered.

Meredith squinted at me. "Are you okay?"

"I'm still pretty shaky," I admitted.

Tyler dropped onto the grass and lowered his head between his knees. "I feel sick," he groaned. "I really do."

"Can't take a joke?" Duffy cried. He shook his head in disgust, turned, and started jogging up the hill.

"It wasn't a joke!" Elizabeth called after him. "It was sick!"

"Let's go complain to Mr. Farraday," Meredith insisted. "I'll bet he doesn't even know what that creep did to us."

"Okay. Let's go," I agreed. "We came here for fun. But so far, it's all been a little too scary."

I helped Tyler to his feet. Then I started to follow Meredith and Elizabeth to the lodge.

But I stopped after a few steps. And stared up into a tall, leafy sassafras tree that rose up above the ride.

"What is that?" I cried. "A camera?"

Yes. All four of us saw it now. A camera perched on a low branch, aimed down at the ride.

"Are we being watched?" I wondered out loud. "Do you think someone taped us as we spun around?"

"Is Mr. Farraday watching us?" Meredith asked, frowning. "Is he filming us?"

"We definitely have to complain," Elizabeth said. "He can't do that to us. This is crazy!"

We climbed the hill to the lodge. I took deep breaths as we walked. I started to feel stronger. The dizziness faded away.

Tyler's normal color returned. His expression remained grim. He clenched his jaw. But I could tell he was feeling a little better.

We passed a row of trash cans along the side of the building. Something caught my eye. A head?

A head poking out from under the lid?

I leaped back as the head moved.

An animal head, I saw now.

A raccoon. It glared up at us, then jumped out of the can and scampered for the trees.

"Whoa," I muttered. "Too many surprises here. Everything is making me jump!"

We entered the lodge and waited for our eyes to adjust to the dim light. Kids were working with clay in an arts and crafts group. As we passed their door, I saw ugly clay masks and monsters.

We stepped past the big meeting room and mess hall. Inside, I glimpsed workers still cleaning up from lunch.

Mr. Farraday's office stood at the end of the long hall. Our sneakers thudded loudly on the wooden floor as we made our way quickly down the hall.

Two green-uniformed counselors passed us, heading the other way. "How's it going?" one of them asked pleasantly.

We didn't reply.

We passed an office marked CAMP ASSISTANT. That must be Alonso's office, I realized.

Another office had the words STAY OUT! stenciled on the door.

Mr. Farraday's office door was closed.

Meredith and Elizabeth hesitated. I raised my fist to knock on the door.

But I left my fist in midair when I heard the first scream.

A shrill scream of panic. Of pain. From inside the office.

Followed by another terrifying scream.

I swallowed hard and turned to the others. "Those screams — they sound *real*," I whispered.

Another scream made me jump back from the door.

Silence now.

The four of us exchanged glances. What should we do? Should we hurry away and pretend we hadn't heard anything? Or should we investigate?

I raised my fist again and knocked on the door.

Silence.

I knocked again.

"Someone is in there," Elizabeth whispered. "Why aren't they answering?"

Before I could reply, the door swung open a crack. "Who is it?" a voice called. Mr. Farraday's voice.

He peered out at us. The door swung open a few inches more.

Mr. Farraday poked his head out.

My mouth dropped open as I stared at him. His face was bright red. Sweat rolled down his forehead. Sweat drenched his beard. He was breathing hard.

"Mr. Farraday?" I started. "Are you okay?"

It took him a while to reply. He forced a smile to his lips and mopped sweat off his forehead with the back of his hand.

"Just . . . cooking up some movie magic," he said.

"Those screams —?" Elizabeth started.

"Sound effects," he answered quickly. He mopped more sweat. "You know, I have a whole library of screams." He snickered. "Screams for any occasion."

He gazed hard at us, as if trying to force us to believe him.

But I didn't believe his explanation. The screams were too real. And he was trembling all over and drenched in sweat.

What was he doing in that office?

I had to know. I reached out — and pushed the door open a bit wider.

All four of us gasped when we saw the two creatures hunkered at the back of the office. Were they human? Were they animals?

They had round, bald heads as green as melons. Tiny black eyes above long lizard snouts. Fat green bodies with bulging bellies.

They lowered their heads and made loud, snuffling sounds as the door swung open. Were they crying?

I gasped again when I saw that their arms and legs were chained, chained to the wall.

Mr. Farraday quickly swung the door back. "You shouldn't have done that, Andrew," he said coldly.

"But — what *are* they?" I choked out.

"Special effects, of course," he replied angrily. "Do you think I keep *real monsters* in my office?"

"Well . . ." I could feel my face turning red.

He narrowed his eyes menacingly. "I don't like snoops and troublemakers," Mr. Farraday said. "You're in Cabin Three, aren't you? Along with those other two troublemakers."

"But — but —" I sputtered.

His eyes glared coldly into mine. "Well, Andrew, you and your brother are in the *lucky* cabin!" he declared. "Yes. You are very lucky indeed."

"Wh-what do you mean?" I stammered.

"You get to find out what Fright Camp is really all about," he replied.

16

"Farraday had to be telling the truth," Meredith said. "Those were movie creatures." She tugged back her hair and tied it with a rubber band. Then she dropped onto the grass beside my cabin.

"Well . . . I never saw those guys in any movie," Tyler argued. "And it didn't look like costumes. They were breathing!"

"If they were just movie monsters, why did Farraday get so angry?" I asked. "Why did he threaten Tyler and me?"

The four of us had hurried away as fast as we could. Of course we never even mentioned Duffy and the Spin-and-Scream.

And now we settled in the shadow of my cabin, trying to calm down, and trying to make sense of what we saw.

The afternoon sun was slowly sinking behind the trees. I could hear happy shouts and cries from swimmers down at the lake.

"If they were just actors in costumes," Tyler said, "why were they chained to the wall? Why did —"

"Why were they screaming?" Meredith interrupted.

"Yes. You heard those screams," her sister added. "They sounded so real. They didn't sound like pretend screams."

"And why was Mr. Farraday so red and out of breath?" Meredith demanded.

I shrugged. "Beats me. I can't answer any of those questions."

"It's all so weird," Tyler murmured.

"Everything about this place is weird," Elizabeth replied. "It's a fright camp, right? I mean, we shouldn't believe anything we see. It's all just supposed to be scary fun."

"That's right," I sighed. "But when does the *fun* start?"

Dinner in the big lodge hall was quiet. A food fight erupted at a table on the far side. But after a few minutes of flying plates of lasagna and salad, the counselors got everyone to calm down.

After the main course, a server tripped and dropped a big metal platter of ice cream dishes. That got everyone cheering and clapping.

We stayed in the lodge and watched one of R.B. Farraday's scariest movies, *The Cavern of No Return.*

Tyler and I owned the video, and we'd watched it at least a dozen times.

In the movie, teenagers go exploring in these big rock caves somewhere out West. They find a huge cavern that looks interesting. They make their way inside and slide down a steep slope, deep, deep into the mouth of the cavern.

They explore for a while. But it's too dark to see anything. So they decide to climb back out. And that's where they run into major trouble.

Because there's no way out.

It really is a Cavern of No Return. And just when the teenagers realize they are trapped in the cavern forever, they start to hear footsteps and weird, rumbling growls. And they realize they are not alone.

Cool plot, huh?

I enjoyed seeing the film on the big screen in the lodge. After the movie, Tyler and I were talking excitedly about what a classic it was as we made our way down the path to our cabin.

A full moon lit our way. The silvery light made the whole campgrounds glow.

Something caught my eye as we reached the first cabin on the path, a girls' cabin. I stopped and squinted up at the slanted roof.

Was that a camera hidden under the eaves?

Yes. Another camera, aimed at the path.

Are there cameras everywhere? I wondered. Is Farraday spying on us all the time? Is he *filming* us?

I pointed it out to Tyler. He yawned. He's not used to staying up so late. "Maybe it's for safety," he suggested.

"Yeah. Safety," I repeated. It made sense. But I didn't believe it.

Later, lying in the top bunk, I couldn't fall asleep.

The light from the full moon made the cabin nearly as bright as during the day. And I kept hearing moans and animal howls outside. Outside but nearby.

I heard Tyler stir in the bunk beneath me. "Andrew, do you hear those howls?" he whispered.

"All part of Fright Camp," I told him. "Just sound effects. There must be a loudspeaker outside the cabin."

"Are you sure?" Jack asked, jumping out of his lower bunk.

Chris lowered himself to the floor. "What's going on? Who's crying out there?"

I slid out of bed and crept to the window. The others followed close behind.

I gazed out onto the silvery grass.

High on the hill I saw two figures. Dark against

the shimmering trees. Squinting hard, I saw them tilt their heads back. Cup their hands around their mouths.

And then they howled. Howled like animals up at the moon.

The creatures from Farraday's office!

"How did they get free?" Tyler asked, tugging my sleeve. "What are they *doing* out there?"

Nobody heard the howling last night — no one except Tyler, me, Chris, and Jack.

No one saw the two creatures high on the hill, standing in the silvery moonlight, howling like animals.

No one — except Cabin Three.

How could that be, I wondered as I grabbed a green towel from the pile and tossed it over my shoulder. Then I made my way along the narrow, sandy beach toward the roped-in swimming area.

I need a swim, I told myself. I'd just finished a seven-inning softball game under the hot sun. I was burning up!

I waved to Tyler. He and several other kids were already in the water. It was his instructional swim period.

The counselor was starting to demonstrate the butterfly stroke. "Watch how I breathe," she said as I passed. "Hey — you're not watching. The hardest part of the butterfly . . ."

Her voice faded behind the gentle lapping of the water.

Wisps of white cloud floated high in the sky. The late morning sun beamed down, warming my shoulders, burning the back of my neck.

I dropped my towel onto the sand and straightened the top of my baggy swimsuit. The lake sparkled brightly, reflecting the sunlight. I squinted at the water, wishing I'd remembered my sunglasses.

I saw some girls swimming out to the floating platform. It bobbed in the water at the back of the roped-in area.

"Hey, Andrew! Andrew!"

I turned at the sound of my name. And saw Meredith and Elizabeth stretched out on beach towels on top of the sand, sunning themselves.

I waved to them, but I didn't go over. I needed a swim. I couldn't wait to cool off.

I turned and started to jog across the hot sand to the water. And nearly ran into Duffy, the big guy from the Spin-and-Scream ride.

"Whooa!" He dodged to the side. He wore a black spandex racing suit. A silver whistle bounced on a chain over his broad chest. His whole body was perfectly tanned and greased up with suntan lotion.

"Welcome to the Lake of the Water Zombies," he greeted me.

"What are *you* doing here?" I blurted out.

"I'm lifeguard this morning," he replied. He slid silver-tinted sunglasses off his forehead, over his eyes. He turned to the water. "Going in?"

I grunted yes and took off.

"If you see any water zombies, just shout!" he called after me.

Was that supposed to be a joke?

Pretty lame, I thought.

I remembered Mr. Farraday's water zombies movie. A bunch of people drown when their ship sinks to the bottom of the ocean. They come back to life as the Swimming Undead and terrorize divers who go down to explore the ship.

Not one of my favorite Farraday films. I don't really like underwater movies. And I really didn't want to think about evil underwater creatures when I was about to take a swim in a lake.

"Breathe! Now . . . breathe!" I could hear my brother's counselor continuing her butterfly lesson.

I took a deep breath and ran into the water. The cold water rose up over my ankles, up my legs. My toes sank into the soft, sandy bottom as I ran.

I ran until the cold water rose up to my waist.

Then I dove under, swimming hard, swimming out, away from the beach.

I bobbed up and took a deep breath. Then I allowed myself to float on the gently rocking waves. Such clear, clean water.

It felt so good. I dove back under. Swam under the surface for a while.

Then I floated up. Pushed my hair back off my forehead. Tilted my face up to the sun.

I lowered my head and started to swim slowly, steadily out to the white floating platform. I was four or five strokes away from it when I felt something wrap around my ankle.

At first, I thought it was a piece of seaweed.

But then I felt it grip me. Cold, hard fingers tightening around my ankle.

Then tugging, tugging me down.

"Hey!" I cried out in protest.

I kicked hard.

I thrashed the water with both hands. I sucked in a deep breath.

"Let go!"

I squirmed and kicked.

But the hard, bony hand held on, tugging me, tugging me underwater.

I shot both hands up, reached up as if trying to grasp the surface.

But I felt myself pulled down. Down . . .

Kicking, thrashing, I spun underwater and saw

it — saw a horrifying figure. All bones and torn skin.

Bones grasping my ankle. Green skin floating loose off the bony chest.

Its head was lowered as it held on to me, pulling me deeper underwater.

I spun and kicked and struggled. My chest felt about to burst.

My heart pounded as I stared through the murky, tossing blue, stared at the undead creature, at the ribbons of flesh floating off the bones.

I thrashed my arms wildly. Bent my knees. Kicked out with all my strength.

But it held on ... held on ...

And then it slowly raised its head to me.

In panic, in cold horror, I stared at the green bloated face.

Stared at it ... stared at it.

Jack's face.

18

My chest bursting, I floated up. Raised my arms and floated to the top.

Overcome with horror, with shock, I didn't feel him let go. I didn't see the bony fingers loosen their grip.

I didn't see the creature back off... the creature with Jack's face.

I shot up to the surface. Burst over the top of the water.

I let out a long whoosh of air. And sucked fresh air in with a gasping breath.

I wanted to scream and breathe at the same time.

I took another deep breath. Then, my heart thudding against my chest, I began to pull myself to the shore. Arms and legs aching, my strokes ragged and frantic, I hurtled over the water.

Desperate to get away . . .

Was he chasing after me?

Was he about to grab me again? Pull me under and not let go this time?

Shivering and shaking, I staggered onto the beach. I spun back to the water, my eyes narrowed, hugging myself tightly.

No sign of him now.

Three girls sunbathing on the floating platform. My brother and his class practicing their new stroke.

No one else.

I turned and tried to walk. My legs felt weak and rubbery. "Duffy?" I searched the beach for him.

Gone. Vanished. Vanished once again.

I opened my mouth in a furious cry.

Was that Duffy's job? To disappear when you really needed him?

I stumbled down the beach, searching for another counselor. "Look out!" I called to my brother's instructor. I cupped my hands around my mouth. "Look out! He's in there!" I cried, pointing to the water. "He's in there!"

She couldn't hear me. My words came out weak and breathless.

Tyler gazed up at me, then quickly returned to practicing his stroke.

"Andrew — are you okay?"

Meredith and Elizabeth came running across

the sand to me. Elizabeth grabbed me by the arm. "What happened? We saw you stagger out."

"You look *awful!*" her sister exclaimed.

They both smelled of coconut suntan lotion. Meredith had a white coating of it on her nose. They studied me, their faces tight with concern.

"He's in there," I murmured. "He . . . grabbed me."

"Huh? Who grabbed you?" Elizabeth demanded.

"He did. A creature," I replied. I pointed to the water. "He's in there."

I knew I wasn't making much sense. I still couldn't think clearly. The sunlight flashed in my eyes like a thousand camera flashes. The beach spun wildly beneath me.

"He had Jack's face," I told them. "But it wasn't Jack. It couldn't be Jack."

"Why not?" Meredith asked. "It probably was Jack playing a joke on you."

"No! It wasn't a joke!" I cried. "He — he tried to drown me! Jack wouldn't try to drown me."

"You've been in the sun too long," Meredith said. "Or something."

"We'll help you to the nurse," Elizabeth offered.

They each took one arm and led me — dripping wet — up the path from the beach. By the time we reached the cabins, my heart stopped racing and I started to feel a little more normal.

"I don't want to go to the nurse," I told them. "I just want to go to my cabin."

"You should at least go tell a counselor," Elizabeth said. "If Jack is playing dangerous games in the lake . . ."

"It wasn't Jack!" I insisted. "It was a . . . creature. I'll tell a counselor. Later. First I want to get dried off. And I want to sit down by myself and think. I have to figure out what's going on here."

We stopped outside my cabin door. I thanked them for helping me up from the beach.

Then I pushed open the door — and let out a startled gasp.

All three of us stared at the message scrawled in red paint on the cabin wall beside my bunk:

THE HORROR IS REAL. GET AWAY — WHILE YOU CAN.

19

Was R.B. Farraday trying to terrify us?

Was it all movie special effects? Or was something really dangerous going on here?

Were the scrawled words a joke — or a desperate warning?

Was my life in danger? Tyler's and Jack's and Chris's lives too?

And where was Jack?

I hadn't seen him all day.

Was that really Jack under the water?

Did Farraday turn him into a water zombie?

Get a grip, I told myself. And I tried. I really did. But I kept hearing Farraday's words: *Cabin Three is the lucky cabin. You'll find out what Fright Camp is really all about.*

I had to talk to someone. I had to get some answers.

At lunch, I searched for Gus, our counselor. But he was nowhere to be found.

So I cornered the first counselor I found in the mess hall. Her name was Claire. She was a tall, friendly-looking sports counselor with frizzy black hair piled up on her head.

"You have to tell me the truth," I demanded. "Is it all real?" I had to shout over the clatter of dishes and the loud voices that echoed across the big room.

Claire led me away from the entrance. "What's wrong?" she asked, placing both hands on my shoulders. "What's upsetting you?"

"Is it real?" I repeated. "The scares, I mean."

She narrowed her eyes at me. "Are you too frightened?"

"Just answer my question!" I screamed. "The electric shock that first day? The guy breaking the Spin-and-Scream? The weird howls at night? And — the creature in the lake. Someone tried to drown me today! A creature!"

Claire studied me. I could see she was trying to decide what to tell me. Then she glanced around, checking to see if anyone was watching.

"Tell me," I insisted. "I have to know what's going on here."

She lowered her head, bringing her face close to

mine. "You heard what Mr. Farraday said," she whispered. "He said he thinks the horror has to be real to be scary."

She glanced tensely up and down the long hall again.

"What does that mean?" I demanded. "Are you saying that was a *real* creature in the lake? Are you saying our lives really are in danger?"

"I — I don't know," she stammered. "I just know . . ."

Her voice trailed off. I followed her eyes. They stared at a camera perched above us in the corner of the hall.

"I can't say any more," she whispered. She turned and ran to the mess hall door.

I started after her. But I stopped when I heard familiar voices just inside the big room.

"You have to call your parents," I heard Chris say.

"No. I can't. I'm too afraid." Jack's reply.

Jack . . . ?

I bolted into the big room.

"You have to call your parents! You can't let them get away with that!" Chris was insisting.

"No way! You know what he'll do to me. He'll —" Jack cut his sentence short as soon as he saw me.

They both stared at me.

I realized I'd interrupted something serious. But I didn't care. "Jack!" I cried. "Was that you? Underwater? Did you pull me under?"

"Excuse me?" Jack squinted at me. "Are you making sense? I don't think so."

"Hel-lo!" Chris knocked on my head. "Anyone in there?"

I shoved his hand away. "Stop fooling around!" I insisted. "You weren't in the lake this morning?" I asked Jack.

"No way," he murmured. "I was flapping my arms and flying to Jupiter."

"Stop joking! I want to know the truth. What's going on here? I know that you two know. You both know. You've got to tell me!"

Jack and Chris exchanged glances.

Then Jack grabbed my shoulder and pulled me closer. He lowered his mouth to my ear. "It's too late," he whispered.

"Huh?" I gasped.

"It's too late," he repeated. "It's already begun. There's nothing we can do about it."

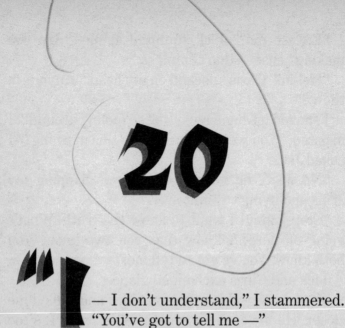

20

"**I** — I don't understand," I stammered. "You've got to tell me —"

I suddenly realized that both boys weren't looking at me any longer. They were staring over my shoulder, staring in fright.

I wheeled around — and saw Alonso hovering over us. His strange gray eyes narrowed. The scar pulsed angrily over his eyebrows.

Chris backed away. "We didn't say anything!" he cried to Alonso.

"We didn't tell him anything. Really!" Jack insisted, his face going white.

"Troublemakers," Alonso muttered through gritted teeth. "I've warned you before."

"No — please!" Jack wailed.

"You have to believe us!" Chris pleaded.

Alonso scowled and waved them away. He

sneered at me. "You get to your table too. Stop causing trouble."

"Huh? Trouble?" I gasped.

"I have my eye on you," Alonso warned. "Cabin Three. The *lucky* cabin." He walked away, laughing.

They served some kind of stew for dinner. I didn't feel much like eating.

I saw Tyler across the room, laughing and joking with some new friends. Meredith and Elizabeth both stopped by my table to ask if I was feeling better.

I said I felt okay. I didn't know what else to say.

I poked a fork at my stew and thought about all that had happened. Fright Camp is supposed to be fun, I told myself. But I wasn't having any fun. I was too scared to enjoy myself.

Was I being a wimp?

No, I decided. There was real danger here. Real horror.

Something evil was taking place here.

I glanced down the table at Jack and Chris. They were eating their dinner, hunched over their plates, eyes down, not speaking to anyone.

They're terrified too, I realized.

They know what's happening in this camp. And they're terrified too.

I wanted to call my parents. I wanted to tell them this camp wasn't working out. To come rescue Tyler and me before something terrible happened.

But they were traveling around Australia all month. I had no idea how to reach them.

I looked up from my plate and saw Alonso stride to the front of the room. "I have an urgent announcement," he boomed.

The big room instantly grew silent.

"Please pay attention," Alonso continued. "The chef is worried that poison mushrooms were accidentally used in the stew. He believes the mushrooms were used on two plates. If your stew tastes funny, please report it immediately."

Laughter burst out around the room.

"Mine tastes funny!"

"Mine tastes weird!"

"Mine tastes like garbage!"

More wild laughter. Hands were shooting up.

"Mine!"

"No — mine!"

Everyone enjoyed the joke.

But Alonso's expression remained grim. "This is no laughing matter," he shouted angrily. "If bad mushrooms were used on two plates, we must find those plates."

"But why did you wait so long?" Elizabeth called out. "We're almost finished eating!"

Alonso opened his mouth to reply.

But before he could get a word out, we all heard a loud groan. And then a gasp of pain.

I turned toward the sound — and saw Jack and Chris grab their stomachs.

Chris struggled to his feet, his eyes wide with horror. He clutched his stomach and doubled over.

Jack uttered a loud groan. "It hurts," he moaned. "Ohhh — my stomach. It *hurts* so bad!"

Both boys doubled over, groaning and clutching their stomachs.

"I think we found the two poisoned plates!" Alonso declared. A strange smile spread over his face.

I don't believe this! I thought.

Jack and Chris poisoned? That's no accident!

I leaped to my feet. "Are you just going to stand there?" I cried to Alonso. "Aren't you going to help them?"

Alonso's smile faded. He shook his head sadly. "I'm afraid it's too late," he said softly.

Everyone cried out as Jack and Chris crumpled to the floor.

21

The big room erupted in cries of panic. Angry shouts.

I jumped to my feet. I'm getting out of here — now! I decided. This place is *sick*!

Counselors were dragging Jack and Chris to a side door. I ran down the long table and grabbed Tyler. "Come on," I said, pulling him to his feet. "We're getting out of here."

He didn't hesitate. We both ran to the front door.

We were only a few feet away when two gray-uniformed guards stepped into the doorway to block our path.

"Whoooa!" Tyler and I stopped short, bumping into each other.

"Guards?" I cried out. "Since when does a camp have guards?"

The two men glared at us coldly and didn't reply.

"We want out of here!" Tyler insisted.

"I don't think so," one of the guards sneered.

Meredith and Elizabeth came running up behind us. "We have to phone our parents — right now!" Elizabeth demanded shrilly.

One of the guards snickered. "That isn't going to happen," he told her flatly.

I totally lost it. I spun around, searching for Alonso. "Are we prisoners here?" I screamed over the shouts and cries of all the other campers. "Are we prisoners?"

The guards herded us back to our cabins. Tyler and I slumped onto our bunks.

A counselor poked his head into the window. "Lights out — now!" he ordered.

I didn't feel like arguing. I turned off the lights.

"What are we going to do?" Tyler asked softly. He leaned back against the wall, hugging himself.

"I don't know," I replied. "Maybe we'll wait till everyone is asleep and —"

"This is just like *Prisoners of the Vampire King*," Tyler said. "Remember that movie? The guards in that film wore gray too."

"I don't care about movies anymore," I replied bitterly. "I'm never going to another R.B. Farraday movie as long as I live."

I heard a soft whirring sound.

Glancing up, I spotted a square object perched on a cabin rafter. I stood up to see it better. A camera. A camera whirring away.

"They're spying on us," I told Tyler.

He stared up at the camera. "Oh, wow," he murmured.

I shook my fist at it angrily. "I don't care!" I cried. "I don't care what you do. We're getting out of here!"

I lowered my gaze to the bunk across the cabin.

The empty bunk.

Tyler followed my stare. "Do you think Jack and Chris are okay?" he asked in a whisper.

I shrugged. "I hope so."

I crossed to the window and stared out. In the silvery moonlight, gray-uniformed guards — at least a dozen of them — patrolled the campgrounds.

"We'll never get anywhere tonight," I told my brother. "Not with those guards out there."

"But we have to try!" Tyler protested.

"Tomorrow morning," I whispered. "Tomorrow morning, we'll find a way to escape."

I didn't get changed. I just pulled off my shoes and climbed under the covers.

After a while, I drifted into a restless sleep. I tossed around, waking up every hour, bits of ugly dreams lingering in my mind.

A scraping sound. A soft *THUD*.

The noises made me open my eyes wide.

I blinked several times. Squinted into the blackness.

I heard another *THUD*. A clunking sound.

A tiny circle of white light darted across the floor.

"Who's in here?" I whispered, my throat clogged from sleep.

I sat up. Someone stumbled heavily across the room.

"Jack? Chris?" I whispered. "Is that you?"

No reply.

A chill made me shiver.

The glowing circle from the flashlight swept over the floor one more time.

"Who's there?" I cried.

The cabin door swung open. The figure moved quickly. Vanished out the door. The door slammed.

I jumped to my feet. And crossed unsteadily to the window.

No one out there now.

I clicked on the lights.

Tyler sat up in his bunk, shaking his head groggily.

"Someone was in here," I told him. "And — and —"

Tyler and I both gasped in shock.

22

"My shoes!" I cried.

I dropped to my knees and reached under the bunk. "Hey!" I lowered myself to the floor and peered underneath.

"My sneakers, my shoes, and my sandals!" I cried, turning to Tyler. "All gone!"

"Mine too," Tyler declared. He shook his head. "I don't believe this."

"He took them all," I murmured. "Someone came into the cabin and took all our shoes."

I heard excited voices outside. I jumped to my feet and ran out to see what was happening.

Kids were pouring out of their cabins. Some were dressed. Some were in pajamas and night-shirts.

"They took my only pair of sneakers!" a boy complained.

"They took my whole bag," a girl wailed. "All my shoes!"

Meredith and Elizabeth hurried over to Tyler and me. "Our shoes," Meredith cried. "Do you believe it?"

"Why did they do this?" Tyler demanded.

"To keep us from escaping," Meredith said. "There's no way we can make it through the woods without any shoes. The ground is crawling with snakes. I heard the counselors say so."

"But — but — but —" Tyler sputtered. "They can't *do* that!"

"*Back to your cabins!*" a guard's voice boomed through a megaphone. "*Thirty seconds to get back to your cabins!*"

Kids were running back and forth in a panic, still talking excitedly about their stolen shoes.

Tyler and I shrank back into the deep shadows beside the cabin. Meredith and Elizabeth followed.

"We're trapped without our shoes," Elizabeth moaned.

"No — we *have* to escape!" a voice cried.

The three of us spun around. Jack and Chris appeared out of the darkness. They both looked really frightened.

"You're okay!" I cried happily.

Chris made a disgusted face. "They pumped our stomachs," he groaned.

"But you're okay!" I repeated.

"Yeah. I guess," Chris replied.

"But we don't have much time. We have to escape," Jack whispered.

"Why? What's going to happen?" I demanded.

Jack and Chris exchanged glances. "We might as well tell them," Chris said. "It's too late now."

Jack turned to us. "Chris and I overheard their plans. We know their secret. That's why they've been picking on us. That's why they chose Cabin Three."

"We're all in danger," Chris added breathlessly. "Meredith and Elizabeth too — because they're your friends."

"But — what?" I demanded. "What are they planning to do?"

"They — they want to scare us to *death*!" Chris exclaimed.

23

"*Fifteen seconds!*" The guard's metal-lic voice through the megaphone made us all jump. "*Back to your cabins — now! Final warning!*"

"They want to scare us to death," Chris re-peated in a whisper. "It's some kind of weird ex-periment or something."

"Does Farraday know about it?" I asked.

Chris shrugged. "We don't know. We only know they're not kidding around. They want to see how much fear a kid can take . . . before he croaks!"

Elizabeth gasped. "But they *can't* do that! Our parents —"

"I called my mom," Jack whispered. "There's a pay phone in the infirmary. I called her. I told her to get here as fast as she can."

"Do you think —" I started.

"She'll be here tomorrow morning," Jack said. "She can save us all." He swallowed hard. "If it isn't too late."

I let out a sigh of relief.

"What are you kids doing out here?" A big, beefy guard lurched around the side of the cabin, his eyes narrowed in anger. *"Get to your cabins — now!"*

Meredith and Elizabeth let out shrieks and took off.

Tyler, Jack, Chris, and I trudged into Cabin Three. I shut the door hard behind me. Our bare feet slapped against the wooden floor. I saw that Jack and Chris had no shoes, either.

On the rafter above us, the camera continued to whir.

"Do you really think your mom can get us out of here?" Tyler asked Jack.

Jack nodded.

I saw a glint of light on the back of his neck. The moonlight reflecting off something.

I stepped over to him to get a closer look.

And gasped when it came into focus.

A small metal chip, implanted in the skin behind his ear.

I spun around — and spotted a chip behind Chris's ear too.

"What did they *do* to you?" I cried. "What are those things they planted in you?"

Jack and Chris both stared back at me blankly. "Things? What things?"

The next morning we walked barefoot across the wet grass to breakfast. A red ball of a sun hung heavily over the trees. Black clouds over the lake darkened the beach below us.

Stern-faced guards watched our every move. Angry and frightened, kids muttered to each other. A camera over the mess hall doorway caught our unhappy expressions as we entered.

Tyler, Meredith, Elizabeth, Chris, Jack, and I sat in a row at the back table, closest to the door. We wanted to be ready to sneak out as soon as Jack's mom arrived.

Silence.

Voices usually rang out through the big room. But this morning, the only sounds were the clatter of spoons against cereal bowls and some sniffling and coughing.

But as soon as Alonso appeared at the front fireplace, the room exploded in voices. He was barraged by angry questions.

"Why did you take our shoes?"

"Are we prisoners? Why do you have guards?"

"Can we call home?"

"Can we leave this camp?"

"Are you going to give us back our shoes?"

"Give us our shoes! Give us our shoes!" Campers at the front table began to shout. And the chant quickly spread over the entire hall.

Alonso stood perfectly still, his face a blank. Finally, he raised both hands above his head for silence.

"We have only borrowed your shoes!" he declared when the chanting stopped and the room finally quieted down. "Your shoes were taken for your own protection."

These words caused another explosion of angry voices.

Once again, Alonso waited for quiet. His face reddened as he waited. The scar on his forehead throbbed.

"We have heard some frightening stories," he explained. "Some frightening things in the woods. We took your shoes to keep you all close. But don't worry. You will get them back when it is safe again."

Alonso continued talking. But his words were drowned out by boos and angry shouts.

He motioned frantically for silence. Someone threw a grapefruit half at him. He ducked. The grapefruit bounced off the stone fireplace.

Kids cheered. Another grapefruit half went flying. Someone tossed a cereal bowl. It smashed against the wall.

Guards rushed to the front of the room to protect Alonso.

Over the shouts and cries, I heard a high scream. A woman's scream. From outside.

I saw Jack's eyes go wide.

"Mom!" he gasped. "That's my mom!"

He leaped away from the table and tore out through the door. Tyler and I scrambled out behind him.

"Mom?" Jack called.

The storm clouds had rolled overhead. I squinted into the gray. It was nearly as dark as night.

"Hellllp!" Another high scream. From near the trees.

"This way!" I cried and began running toward the sound.

I saw two green-uniformed counselors running full speed — in the other direction.

"Hellllp me!" Jack's mom shrieked.

Jack spotted her first. "She — she's in the quicksand pit! Did they throw her in? *Did* they?"

"Jack — get help!" she cried. She flailed both arms above her head.

The sand was up over her waist. She was sinking fast.

Jack started to run to her.

"No!" I cried. I grabbed his shoulders and jerked him back. "You'll sink too!"

"Get a rope!" Elizabeth shrieked. "Get a tree branch! Something for her to hold on to!"

"Help me. I'm . . . going down!" Jack's mom wailed. She stabbed at the sand frantically with both hands. Grasping handfuls. Struggling desperately for something to hold her up.

"Hurry! Hurry!" she cried. The sand rose up to her chest.

"Get help! Get help!" Tyler cried.

I had an idea. "I'm going to get Mr. Farraday!" I told them. I spun back to the main lodge. "He'll help us. I know he will!"

"Just *hurry!*" Jack's mom pleaded.

I heard a rumble of thunder as I took off toward the lodge. Gasping for breath, I burst past a guard at the door and turned down the long hall.

"Hey, wait —" he called after me.

But I was already halfway to Mr. Farraday's office at the end of the hall.

"Mr. Farraday! Mr. Farraday!" I called his name as I ran. "We need help!"

The office door stood open. He had to be in there. He *had* to.

I grabbed the sides of the doorway — and pushed myself inside.

"Mr. Farraday?" I called breathlessly.

No. Not at his desk.

"Mr. Farraday?"

I heard the sound of a car starting up. The window stood open. The curtains fluttered in a gusting wind.

A rumble of thunder. And then the roar of a car engine.

I dove to the window. Leaning on the ledge, I poked my head out.

And saw a black car squealing away, tires spinning over the dirt path. Mr. Farraday's car!

I could see him hunched forward, both hands on the top of the wheel. Roaring down the hill, away from the camp.

"Hey! Where are you going?" I called after him. But of course he couldn't hear.

With a sigh, I ducked back into the office. I started to the door — when something on his desk caught my eye.

A note. A handwritten note.

My hand shook as I grabbed it off the desk and read it aloud:

"I can't do this. I can't do this to these kids. I feel so guilty. I'm so sorry. Good-bye, everyone."

"**H**uh?" I gaped at the words until they blurred in front of my eyes. Then I let the note fall to the desk.

I turned to the door — and gasped.

"Reading other people's mail?" Alonso asked, a leering smile on his face. "You know that isn't right, Andrew."

He had dark stains over the front of his white lab coat. He moved quickly to block the door.

"Jack's mom —" I choked out. "You've got to hurry."

"Too late," he said softly.

"No!" I screamed.

"We don't like uninvited guests at Fright Camp," Alonso said.

"No! That's horrible!" I cried.

Alonso stepped aside. Two guards moved

quickly into the room and grabbed me by the shoulders.

I thrashed and squirmed and tried to struggle free. But they were too strong.

They started to drag me out of the office. I spotted a camera aimed down at us from a high bookshelf.

"What is that camera for?" I asked Alonso. "Why are there cameras all over the camp?"

"Don't ask any more questions," he replied coldly. "You've already seen too much."

They pulled me out into the hall. "Where are you taking me?" I demanded.

"To join your brother and the other troublemakers," Alonso said. "They're waiting for you, Andrew. In a place you'll find very interesting."

"Are they okay?" I cried. "Is everyone okay?"

Alonso didn't answer.

He led the way into the woods. The guards gripped my arms tightly. We followed a path I'd never seen before. "Watch out for the snakes, Andrew." Alonso grinned.

A cold rain came down, drenching my hair and the sleeves of my T-shirt. I trained my eyes on the ground, looking for snakes. I listened hard for hissing or rattling, but the rain drowned out any sounds.

Alonso shoved me ahead of him on the path. It led up to a dark rock cliff. Cut into the cliff, I saw a small opening. A cave. Totally black inside.

A wooden sign tilted near the cave opening: MINE OF LOST SOULS.

"What is this place?" I asked Alonso. "Am I going in there?"

He nodded. "Your friends are already inside, Andrew. They're waiting for you."

The guards forced me up to the opening.

"But what's in there?" I demanded. "Why do we have to go in?"

The only reply I received was a hard push.

I stumbled into the darkness. A sharp rock scratched my bare foot.

I tumbled down.

Started to fall.

Slid . . . slid . . .

Down into the blackness.

Down . . . rolling as I fell . . . down . . .

Deeper and deeper . . . into an endless, bottomless hole.

My screams followed me all the way down.

"Ooooof!" I landed hard on my side. A cold, hard floor. The floor of a mine shaft, I realized.

I pulled myself up to my knees. I blinked several times, trying to blink away the darkness. But I was surrounded by solid black. I couldn't see a thing.

I shivered. The air felt cold. And damp.

"Hello?" I called weakly. My voice echoed around the deep cavern. "Anyone down here?"

"Andrew? Is that you?" My brother's voice from somewhere in front of me.

"Tyler? Are you okay?"

A hand bumped me. Slid across my face. Landed on my throat. "Andrew? It's me," Tyler uttered in a tiny, trembling voice. "Are you okay? They threw you down here too?"

"Yes," I told him. I squeezed his cold, wet hand. "Who else is down here?"

"We all are," Elizabeth replied. "My sister and I, Jack and Chris —"

"Jack — your mom!" I choked out.

"I know," he whispered. "Chris and I tried to save her. But —"

He stopped short.

A low growl from somewhere close made us all gasp.

A low, animal growl.

"Oh, noooo," I moaned. My heart skipped a beat. My knees started to buckle.

We're not alone down here, I realized.

We're not alone. . . .

26

We all cried out at the next low growl. Closer this time. Angrier.

"What . . . is . . . that?" I choked out. My heart beat so hard, my head throbbed. I couldn't think straight.

"It sounds . . . hungry!" Tyler gasped.

"It's so dark," Jack whispered. "If only we could see something."

"Whoa. Wait," Chris murmured. "I have a plastic lighter in my pocket. One of the counselors dropped it. Hold on."

I held my breath. I tried to force my legs to stop trembling.

I waited for the flicker of Chris's lighter.

"Owww!" I let out a shrill cry as bright lights flashed on.

I squeezed my eyes shut. Then opened them slowly.

And stared at Mr. Farraday, grinning across a crowded room at us.

We weren't in an empty mine shaft. We were standing in a large, round room filled with counselors and guards. They sat in folding chairs — and all burst into applause as my startled brother and friends and I gaped openmouthed at them.

Mr. Farraday clapped too, grinning and nodding his head. "Wonderful! That was wonderful!" he declared.

I shook my head hard. Was this a *dream*? I felt too confused to say anything.

"You kids were perfect!" Mr. Farraday declared. He rushed up and started pumping our hands. "Wonderful! Wonderful! You were all so *terrified.*"

The counselors and guards gave us another round of applause.

Mr. Farraday turned to Alonso, who was standing against the back wall. "Are the cameras still running? You can turn them off now."

Then the movie director swung back to us. "Let's give special thanks to the actors who played Jack and Chris!" he exclaimed.

"Huh? Actors?" I cried, even more confused.

More applause.

Jack and Chris took bows.

"Wonderful job, boys," Mr. Farraday congratulated them. "You really fooled everyone. You were perfect campers. No one guessed that you were staff members, working for me."

I grabbed Jack's arm. "You're an actor?"

He nodded, grinning at me.

"And none of that stuff was real?" I demanded. "The electric shock? The food poisoning?"

His grin grew wider. "You're catching on, Andrew."

"The creature in the lake?" I cried. "The one with your face?"

"A costume. I waited behind the floating platform for you."

He pulled the little chip out from behind his ear. "It's a microphone," he told me. "That's how I got my instructions from Mr. Farraday."

"Didn't you wonder why all the terrible things were happening to us guys in Cabin Three?" the actor who played Chris asked. "We were all set up to frighten whoever ended up in the *lucky* cabin!"

"And I also want to thank Max, who played the part of Duffy," Mr. Farraday continued. More applause. "And a special thanks to Margo, who played Jack's mom. Great job in the quicksand pit, Margo."

Mr. Farraday turned to the back of the room. "And a special thanks to my brother Ned, who played the part of Alonso."

More applause as Alonso — or Ned — took a bow.

"Hey — what's the big idea?" I cried angrily. "Why did you do this to us?"

"Why did you trick us?" Elizabeth demanded.

Mr. Farraday crossed the room. He put an arm around my shoulder and his other arm around Elizabeth's shoulder. "You are in my new movie," he announced. "My first documentary."

"But — but —" Tyler sputtered.

Mr. Farraday continued. "You probably saw the cameras around camp. I wanted to capture *real* terror on film. Not movie terror — but *real* terror. I wanted to use all my tricks to frighten you. To scare you out of your minds. I wanted it to be *real. Real!* And it worked. You were wonderful."

I shoved his arm away and spun around to face him. Anger rose up from my chest and burst out in a furious cry. "It was all a fake?" I shrieked. "You frightened us like that — just for a movie? Nothing was real?"

Mr. Farraday's smile faded. He rubbed his beard. "Well ... actually, Andrew, some things here *are* real."

"What?" I demanded. "What is real?"

"It's not important," he replied sharply. "The important thing is, I captured your fear on film. You're going to be famous!"

"But it wasn't fair!" Elizabeth chimed in. "You should have warned us!"

105

Tyler and Meredith agreed. All four of us began angrily shouting at once.

Mr. Farraday raised a hand to silence us. "Calm down, everyone. Now you kids can relax and have fun. Enjoy the camp. You've earned it."

Tyler, Meredith, Elizabeth, and I hurried out. We returned to our cabins. Changed into swimsuits. And took a long, cool swim in the lake.

The camp looked entirely different to me now. The quicksand pit . . . the Cavern of No Return . . . the Haunted Forest . . . None of it seemed scary anymore.

Now I knew the secret. It was all like a movie set. All pretend . . . built so that Mr. Farraday could film our fear.

"I'm still angry," I told the others as we dried off on the beach. "That guy who played Jack nearly drowned me, pulling me under in that gross costume."

"I'm angry too," Meredith agreed. "It wasn't fair. We came here to have fun."

"He *used* us!" Elizabeth declared.

Tyler wrapped himself in a beach towel. He shivered. "It was *too* scary," he said. "It's like we were . . . victims. We never had a chance."

We huddled on the beach and talked about it for a long time. All four of us couldn't calm down. We felt angry and upset.

"We have to make a protest," I said finally. "Farraday and the others don't have the right to scare us like that. They went too far. We have to let people know what he did to us."

The others cheered.

A shadow slid over us.

I turned and saw Ned, Mr. Farraday's brother, watching us from the rocks above the sand.

Did he hear what I was saying?

I felt a chill as I gazed up at him. His strange gray eyes narrowed coldly. The scar on his forehead throbbed.

The scary stuff is over, I thought.

Why is he staring at us like that?

After lunch, we spent the afternoon having fun. We raced the go-carts over the trail that stretched along the trees. The trail was bumpy and filled with rocks. We practically flew over it, shrieking and screaming our heads off with each bump.

We rode the Spin-and-Scream until we were so dizzy we couldn't stop laughing.

We sailed Sunfishes out on the lake. Then we tried windsurfing, which is a lot harder than it looks. After a late-afternoon swim, we headed back to the cabins to get changed for dinner.

Kids were already gobbling down hot dogs and baked beans when I arrived at the mess hall. Some of them glanced up as I walked in. A few clapped and cheered. Others flashed me a thumbs-up.

I guessed that the story of the Lucky Cabin had gotten around.

I grabbed a plate and walked up to the hot dog line. As I waited, I searched for Jack and Chris. But of course they weren't at their usual places. Mr. Farraday had probably paid them for their acting jobs, and they had left camp.

Mr. Farraday waved at me from the front table. He sat surrounded by counselors. His brother Ned sat at the far end of their table, leaning over a plate piled high with food.

I took a seat across from Meredith. She was talking to another girl from her cabin.

I was halfway through my second hot dog when I jumped to my feet. "Hey — where's my brother?" I shouted.

I saw Mr. Farraday turn toward me.

"Where's Tyler?" I cried. "He was right behind me." I called his name several times.

The room grew quiet. "Is there a problem, Andrew?" Mr. Farraday asked.

"My brother," I replied. "He told me he was starving. But he isn't here."

"Maybe he's still in your cabin?" Ned suggested.

I started to the door. "I'll go check. This is weird!"

"Uh . . . Don't be upset. I'll go with you," Mr. Farraday offered.

He hurried across the room to catch up to me. I

led the way down the path to the cabin. I stopped short when I saw the cabin door hanging open.

Mr. Farraday and I hurried up to the open doorway.

"Oh, noooo!" I let out a cry. "What a mess!"

The cabin had been trashed. Blankets and sheets had been pulled off the bunks and crumpled over the floor. One dresser lay on its side, clothes pouring out of the drawers. One window screen had a big hole ripped in it.

Mr. Farraday gasped and raised both hands to his face.

"It — it looks like there was a fight!" I exclaimed in a trembling voice.

"Stay calm. Stay calm," Mr. Farraday instructed. "I'm sure everything is okay. I —"

"Oh, no!" I pushed past him into the cabin. I bent to the floor and picked up an object from under our bed.

I held it up to Mr. Farraday. "My brother's watch!" I cried in horror. "He — he never takes it off! Never!"

"I — I don't understand this," Mr. Farraday stammered. "This shouldn't be happening. The filming is over."

"Then where is my brother?" I shrieked.

28

Mr. Farraday swallowed hard. "I — I don't know who did this," he murmured, staring at the mess. "We'll split up and search for him. He's got to be nearby."

He blew his whistle. Several counselors came trotting down the hill from the mess hall and returned our sneakers.

"Maybe Tyler wandered down to the quicksand pit," I suggested in a tiny voice.

Mr. Farraday shook his head. "It isn't really quicksand. It's just a pile of sand we spread out."

He turned to the counselors. "Search the camp for Tyler, his brother," he instructed them.

But before they could move, Meredith appeared. Her hair was wild around her face. Her features were tight with fear.

"My sister is gone too!" Meredith wailed. "I

thought she was in our cabin — but she isn't. I haven't seen Elizabeth since we left the beach!"

Mr. Farraday put a hand on her trembling shoulder. "Whoa. Stay calm. Everybody, take a deep breath. I'll bet Tyler and Elizabeth are both down at the beach."

The director was trying to sound calm. But I could see the flash of fear in his eyes. His upper lip trembled. He bit down on it to stop it.

He half ran, half walked down the path to the beach. Meredith and I hurried after him.

The cabins were all dark. A steady breeze made the tall grass whisper as we raced by.

In the gray evening light, I could see that the beach was empty.

Meredith let out a sob. She ran ahead of Mr. Farraday, her sneakers kicking up sand.

"It's getting dark," Farraday said, his eyes searching the beach. "Hard to see if —"

Meredith's scream interrupted him.

"Look!" she cried. She bent down and picked something off the sand.

"Huh?" Mr. Farraday uttered a gasp.

"It's Elizabeth's swimsuit!" Meredith wailed.

Mr. Farraday's mouth dropped open.

"It's hers! It's hers!" Meredith shrieked at the top of her lungs. She waved the swimsuit in the air. "Where is she? Where is my sister?"

We all looked out to the water. The lake shimmered darkly in the evening light.

"This can't be happening," Mr. Farraday moaned, shaking his head. He took a deep breath. "Let's get back to the lodge. Maybe someone has seen Elizabeth and Tyler."

"Where is she? What happened to her?" Meredith cried as we made our way back up the hill.

"I'll phone the town police," Mr. Farraday promised. "I don't want you kids to worry. We'll —"

We all stopped when we saw the Spin-and-Scream ride going.

The cars were spinning slowly, creaking and squeaking as they spun.

"Who turned that thing on?" Mr. Farraday demanded. "What is going on around here?"

We jogged toward the whirling ride.

"There's Tyler!" I cried, pointing to one of the cars. "Look! There he is! Tyler! Tyler!"

Mr. Farraday grabbed the lever and pulled it up.

The cars rolled slowly to a stop.

All three of us ran across the grass to the car.

"Tyler?" I called. "Tyler?"

No. Not Tyler.

We stared down in horror at Tyler's *clothes*, spread over the seat.

29

r. Farraday opened his mouth in a gurgling sound. He staggered back, away from the car.

Meredith grabbed Mr. Farraday by the arm and started to shake him wildly. "Stop it! Stop it!" she cried. "You're still trying to scare us! You're still making your stupid movie!"

"No — no, I'm not!" Mr. Farraday insisted. He pulled free of her grasp. "Trust me, Meredith. I'm through filming. I — I don't know *who* is doing this!"

"Well, what are we going to do?" I demanded. "Tyler and Elizabeth wouldn't just wander away."

Mr. Farraday began trotting to the lodge. "I'm going to call the police," he said. "This is real. It isn't a movie."

"We'll come with you," I said.

We followed him into the lodge. Dinner was over. The movie screen had been set up, and the rest of the kids were watching one of Mr. Farraday's movies. I saw the giant insects as we passed the main hall and recognized the movie, *Night of the June Bugs*.

Meredith and I were definitely not in the mood for a horror movie.

Mr. Farraday clicked on his office light, and we followed him inside.

"Sit down, kids." He motioned to the two chairs across from his desk.

"I'm sure the town police will help us." He picked up the phone receiver and raised it to his ear.

"Hey!" He held the receiver out and looked at it. Then he punched several buttons. Then he listened again.

When he raised his eyes to us, his whole body trembled in panic. "The phone is dead," he choked out.

He slumped into his desk chair. "Who is *doing* this?"

30

"Try another phone!" I cried. "Try *something*! We have to get help!"

Two counselors burst into the office. "I — I think we found them!" one of them cried breathlessly.

"Where?" I cried.

"We heard voices," the other one said, struggling to catch his breath. "From down in the Cavern of No Return!"

"But that's impossible!" Mr. Farraday exclaimed. "How did they get down in the cavern? Who put them there?"

"We've got to get them out!" I cried.

A large figure came hurrying down the hall toward us. I recognized Ned, still wearing the stained white lab coat. "What's going on?" he asked his brother.

"Just grab some flashlights," Mr. Farraday replied. "We're going to the cavern."

Ned's mouth dropped open in surprise. Then he spun around and lumbered off to get the flashlights.

A few minutes later, we were making our way quickly through the trees, our flashlights dancing over the ground in front of us. The Cavern of No Return was cut into a rock wall, hidden deep in the woods.

There was no path. So we had to step over fallen tree limbs and push our way through thick tangles of vines and tall weeds. Crickets chirped noisily. All around, I could hear animals scampering over crackling, dead leaves.

Finally, the cavern rose up darkly ahead of us. The mouth of the cavern was a small hole, cut low, only a foot or two high.

We dropped to our knees in front of it.

Mr. Farraday hesitated. "This is too dangerous. We really shouldn't go in there."

"Dangerous?" Meredith cried. "I don't care! My sister is in there! We have to find her!"

"You don't understand —" Ned began.

I turned and lowered myself into the opening. "I'm going to find Tyler!" I declared.

"No. Wait —" Mr. Farraday insisted.

Too late. I slid into the blackness. "Whoooa!" I cried out as I began to tumble down a steep path, down, down into the cavern.

I caught my balance and stumbled down to the cavern floor. My shallow breaths rose up loudly, echoing against the stone walls.

A few seconds later, I saw darting yellow circles of light as Ned, Meredith, and Mr. Farraday made their way down into the cavern.

A chill swept down my back. Despite the summer heat outside, it was *cold* down here.

Mr. Farraday bumped into me. "Oh. Sorry," he muttered. Even in the dim glow of the flashlights, I could see the terrified expression on his face.

"Who — who's down here?" he stammered. "Is anyone here? Tyler? Elizabeth? Are you down here?"

heard a soft moan from somewhere ahead of us.

Mr. Farraday jumped. He heard it too.

A soft cry.

"Who's here?" Mr. Farraday gasped. "Please! Who is it?"

Lights flashed on above us.

We all blinked in the bright light.

Tyler and Elizabeth stood against the wall, both dressed in jeans and Fright Camp sweatshirts.

"Surprise!" they both cried. And burst out laughing.

Meredith and I laughed too.

Mr. Farraday and Ned staggered back, their mouths open, eyes bulging.

"We paid you back!" Meredith exclaimed. She slapped her sister a high five.

"You mean — you mean — you *staged* this whole thing?" Mr. Farraday cried. "Elizabeth and Tyler didn't disappear?"

"It was all a . . . fake?" Ned asked weakly.

We all laughed again. What an awesome moment!

"Yes, we planned the whole thing. Now you know what it feels like to be *really* terrified!" I told them.

"Too bad *we* don't have a camera!" Elizabeth cried. "We could make our own movie about fear!"

We laughed again. We congratulated each other. We were so happy our plan had worked. We felt so good.

"We scared the Scariest Man on Earth!" I cried gleefully.

But then I caught the worried expressions on the faces of the two men. Mr. Farraday had his head tilted, as if he were listening for something.

I guess the great horror director doesn't like it when someone tries to terrify *him*, I decided.

"Mr. Farraday?" I started.

"Ssssh." He held a finger up to his lips. "Listen . . ."

We stopped our celebration and listened. I heard a low buzz, rising and falling.

"What is that?" I asked.

Mr. Farraday still had his finger to his lips.

The buzzing grew nearer. Louder. Rising and falling like a low, droning siren.

"What's that noise?" I asked again.

Tyler, Meredith, and Elizabeth huddled close.

Farraday rubbed his beard tensely. He shut his eyes. "Remember when I said some things here at camp were real?" he asked in a whisper.

I struggled to hear him over the rising buzz.

"This cavern is a giant wasps' nest," he continued. "The wasps and hornets all swarm here at night."

I started toward the opening. I opened my mouth to say, "Let's get out of here!" But panic gripped my throat.

"Let's climb out of here!" Meredith said it for me.

"Can't," Mr. Farraday said flatly. "The climb is too steep."

"It's the Cavern of No Return — remember?" Ned chimed in. "We're trapped down here until someone comes to rescue us."

"Trapped with them . . ." Mr. Farraday added, motioning toward the buzzing.

Louder . . . louder . . .

"Pretend time is over. Now we're going to face *real* terror," Mr. Farraday said softly, shaking his head.

"No!" I protested. "We've got to get out! We can't!"

I had to shout over the rising buzz of the wasp swarms.

My legs trembling, I started to back up. To back away from them. Back . . . back . . .

I tripped over something. Stumbled backwards.

"Hey!"

I scrambled to my knees. And stared at the loudspeaker I'd tripped over.

Loudspeaker?

I raised it to my ear. And heard the buzzing sound pouring out of it.

Sound effects.

Sound effects!

My heart still pounding, I turned back to Mr. Farraday.

He grinned down at me, a gleeful, triumphant grin. "Are you enjoying Fright Camp?" he asked. "Just think — you have two more weeks!"

About R.L. Stine

R.L. Stine is the most popular author in America. He is the creator of the *Goosebumps, Give Yourself Goosebumps, Fear Street*, and *Ghosts of Fear Street* series, among other popular books. He has written nearly 200 scary novels for kids. Bob lives in New York City with his wife, Jane, teen-age son, Matt, and dog, Nadine.

Welcome to the new millennium of fear

Check out this
chilling preview of
what's next from
R.L. STINE

ARE YOU
TERRIFIED YET?

10

Brad pushed back his spiky black hair and grinned at me, a truly evil grin.

I still had the popcorn bowl in my hand. Travis grabbed a handful and stuffed it into his mouth.

"Hi, C-C-C-Craig," David, a chubby, red-haired boy from my class, said. Frankie and Gus, the other two boys, giggled.

My stomach churned. I suddenly felt cold all over.

"Wh-why are you calling me that?" I demanded angrily. (As if I didn't know.)

"My cousin Pam goes to your school," Travis replied. Popcorn kernels dribbled out of his mouth, onto his chin. He grabbed another handful from my bowl.

I shoved the bowl into his hands. "So? What about her?" I asked, trying to sound tough.

Travis chewed for a while. "She told me about you," he said finally. "She told me *all* about you, C-C-C-Craig. She said you were always scared of your own shadow."

I stared at him. I didn't know what to say.

"She told me you screamed your head off and ran away from a chipmunk last year," Travis said, snickering.

Yes. That was true. But it was a *very big* chipmunk.

"That's a lie," I said.

"It's all a big lie!" Amy chimed in. She glared at Travis and his friends. "None of it is true. You're making it all up because you're jealous of Craig."

Brad turned to me. "Is it true?" he demanded. "Is it true that the kids at your old school called you C-C-C-Craig?"

Amy stared at me. The five guys stared at me.

I took a deep breath. "Of *course* it isn't true," I told them. I shook my head. "Why would someone make up such a dumb story? I don't get it."

Brad's evil grin grew wider. His dark eyes gleamed. "Well . . . we'll see," he said softly.

"We'll see who is telling the truth," Travis added. He set the empty popcorn bowl on a table. "We brought a little test for you, Craig."

Uh-oh.

Lightning flashed in the window. I gritted my teeth and waited for the boom of thunder that followed.

"Test?" I asked. I didn't realize I was backing up, backing away from them. I didn't realize it until I backed into the living room couch and nearly fell over.

They followed me into the living room. Amy eyed them suspiciously. "What kind of test?" she demanded.

"David has it," Travis announced. He turned to his friend.

"I kept it dry, under my jacket," David said. He reached under his jacket — and pulled out a tall glass jar.

"Wh-what is it?" I stammered.

David handed the jar to Travis. Travis raised it in front of my face.

And I let out a horrified gasp.

piders.

Ugly, black, hairy-legged spiders. Dozens of them. Crawling all over each other.

Travis pushed the jar against my nose. The spiders blurred into a wriggling pile of black furry bodies and legs.

Amy grabbed the jar away and inspected it. "Where did you find these?" she snapped at Travis. "In your bed?"

The boys all laughed.

I couldn't laugh. I felt like choking. Or fainting. I'm scared of bugs — and spiders are my worst nightmare.

"You told us to bring Craig a test," Brad said to Amy. "So, here it is."

I couldn't take my eyes off the strange, hairy

black spiders scrabbling over each other, an endless wrestling match.

Do they bite? I wondered. Do they pinch? Are they poisonous?

"What do I have to do?" I choked out, trying not to sound frightened. But my voice came out tiny and weak.

"It's simple," Travis replied. "Just keep your hand in the jar for five minutes."

Huh?

"No problem!" Amy sneered. "Craig will keep his hand in there all day! He's not afraid of spiders!"

Amy, please — shut up! I thought.

I stared at the spiders. Then I gazed up at Travis. "Am I allowed to wear gloves?" I asked.

They all burst out laughing. Amy too.

They thought I was joking.

I can't do this, I realized. I'll *die*.

"How much are we betting?" Amy demanded.

"How about a million dollars?" David suggested.

Everyone laughed again.

"I don't have a million dollars," Amy replied. "Let's make a real bet, guys. I can't wait to take your money."

"How about thirty dollars?" Brad suggested.

I gazed into the jar. The black spiders climbed and wrestled. Were they *biting* each other?

Amy and I are going to lose thirty dollars, I thought miserably.

No way we can win. There's no way I can do this.

I tapped her shoulder. I tried to stop her. But she quickly agreed to the bet. "Okay. Thirty dollars. But this is too easy. Why didn't you think of something hard?"

Amy — please shut up! I thought again. I was gritting my teeth so hard, my jaw ached.

How can I get out of this? I wondered. Should I just run out the front door and never come back?

Should I tell them the truth? That I really am C-C-C-Craig?

No. No way, I decided.

I can't let Amy down. I can't let *myself* down.

If I don't try this, I'll be C-C-C-Craig for the rest of my life.

Travis slid open the metal top of the jar. He turned to his friends. "Who has a watch?"

"I do," Brad replied, holding his wrist close to his face. "I'll keep time."

Travis raised the jar to me. "Five minutes," he said, his expression turning solemn.

I gazed into the jar. "Is that Eastern Standard Time?" I joked.

Travis nodded. "Five minutes in the jar." The boys clustered tight around me, eager to have a good view.

Amy pushed her way into the middle. She flashed me a thumbs-up.

Brad had his eyes on his watch. "Ready. Set. *Go!*"

I took a deep breath. My hand was trembling so hard I wasn't sure I could slide it into the jar.

The glass felt cool against the back of my hand. Shutting my eyes, I plunged my hand down . . . down into the jar.

I was okay for a few seconds.

But then I felt a prickling sensation on the back of my hand. I opened my eyes and saw spiders crawling over my skin.

A moan escaped my throat. I tried to stop it, but I couldn't. I forced a smile to my face to cover it up.

I could feel sweat dripping down my forehead. Could the others see it?

They all had their eyes on my hand in the jar.

Spiders prickled my palm. I felt a few of them drag their hairy, dry bodies over my wrist.

"Thirty seconds," Brad announced.

It felt like thirty years!

At least a dozen spiders clung to my hand now. My arm began to itch. My chest itched. My whole body prickled and itched.

I kept the smile frozen on my face. But I couldn't breathe. I couldn't move.

"One minute," Brad called out.

"Four minutes to go," Travis said, leaning his head closer, grinning as he stared into the jar.

I can't do it, I realized.

Enough.

I can't take any more.

I lose. I lose the bet. I lose everything.

Spiders danced over the back of my palm. Sharp legs pinched my wrist. Two of them were scuttling up my arm!

That's all. Good-bye, I decided.

I jerked my hand up. Raised it quickly to pull it from the jar.

But I couldn't remove it.

My hand was stuck — stuck inside the jar.

PREPARE TO BE SCARED!

Goosebumps
SERIES 2000
R.L. STINE

$3.99 Each!

- ☐ BCY39988-8   **#1: Cry of the Cat**
- ☐ BCY39990-X   **#2: Bride of the Living Dummy**
- ☐ BCY39989-6   **#3: Creature Teacher**
- ☐ BCY39991-8   **#4: Invasion of the Body Squeezers (Part I)**
- ☐ BCY39992-6   **#5: Invasion of the Body Squeezers (Part II)**
- ☐ BCY39993-4   **#6: I Am Your Evil Twin**
- ☐ BCY39994-2   **#7: Revenge R Us**
- ☐ BCY39995-0   **#8: Fright Camp**

Log on for Scares!

Scholastic presents

Goosebumps
ON THE WEB!

http://www.scholastic.com/Goosebumps

Something Evil, Something Cruel

"My cousin Justin warned me to stay away from Uncle Clyde's shed. 'I me
it,' he said. 'Don't go in there. Whatever you do.' I knew this had to be
another of Justin's dumb jokes. So I waited until it got dark. Then I crept o
to the shed. I wish I'd never opened that door. But I did. And now I'll neve
be the same. Because this is what I found..."

THE PRIZES!

THE STORY STARTER!

1 Grand Prize Winner will be awarded:

- A trip to scary New Orleans to visit creepy
  graveyards, spooky mansions, and scary
  swamps!
- A DreamWorks Goosebumps
  CD-ROM
- A signed copy of R.L. Stine's
  autobiography, *It Came from Ohio*

Don't Forget!

Look for the Creepstakes clue words each
month this summer (May through August)

- On back-of-book ads in Goosebumps Series
  2000 Books #6 - #9!
- On in-store displays and giveaways!
- On the Goosebumps web site
  (http://www.scholastic.com/goosebumps)

25 First Prize Winners will be awarded:
- A DreamWorks Goosebumps CD-ROM
- A signed copy of *It Came from Ohio*

50 Second Prize Winners will be awarded:
- A signed copy of *It Came from Ohio*

THE RULES!